Praise for *Dog Eat Dog*:

"It makes a wonderful change to read a novel in a setting that I as a black South African can identify with, looking at the struggles that many of us have faced and over-come, and I'm looking forward to Mhlongo's next book."

SIPOKAZI MAPOZA, *Cape Argus*

"Niq is one of many young, fresh and inspiring writers in South Africa today."   DIKATSO MAMETSE, *Drum*

"Mhlongo's work is witty and clever and has no pre-tensions of being a new work for a new democracy – it simply is. A tale that emerges from the heart of his dis-consolate being, it reverberates."

MAUREEN ISAACSON, *Sunday Independent*

"Mhlongo uses his witty, gritty and vibrant style to ad-dress issues such as safe sex, Aids, xenophobia, poverty and the challenges young people continue to face in the new South Africa."   IDO LEKOTA, *Sowetan*

"Street-wise and pregnant with teenage wit, the book is pacy and musical."

BONGANI MADONDO, *Sunday Times*

"This debut novel has a hard-hitting realism and a punchy racial and political shrewdness that's difficult to ignore. A vibrant read."   *wordonthestreet, Y Mag*

"There are moments of real emotional power inter-mingled with darkly humorous escapades . . . a potential trendsetter."   LARA SCOTT, *African Review of Books*

NIQ MHLONGO

After Tears

KWELA BOOKS

Kwela Books,
an imprint of NB Publishers,
40 Heerengracht, Cape Town, South Africa
PO Box 6525, Roggebaai, 8012, South Africa
http://www.kwela.com

Model on cover: Arthur Sishube
Cover photographer: Antonia Steyn
Cover design: Johan van Wyk
Typography: Nazli Jacobs
Set in Bookman
Printed and bound by Paarl Print,
Oosterland Street, Paarl, South Africa

First edition, first impression 2007
Second impression 2008

ISBN-10: 0-7957-0256-6
ISBN-13: 978-07957-0256-3

In memory of my best friends:

Moses Kgoale (1973 – 1997) and

Daniel Armstrong Mabasa (1969 – 2005)

RIP

ONE
November 22, 1999

That was it. I had had enough of Cape Town. The cold Atlantic Ocean, the white sand beaches, Table Mountain, the Waterfront, everything I had once found so beautiful about the city, had suddenly turned ugly. I decided right there, in front of the notice board, to go and pack my belongings and leave for good. The compass in my mind was pointing north, back to Johannesburg, my landlocked city, and Soweto. I was sure that if I stayed in Cape Town for one more day I would go mad. The four years that I had spent there, shuttling between the university lecture theatres and libraries, had come to nil. My fate had been decided. I wasn't fit to become an advocate the following year. I was a failure.

* * *

My eyes were burning as the morning started to break. My muscles were stiff and my neck was aching. I knew that I had to be awake at every single station the train came to a halt at as my lady friend Vee had warned me of the dangers of falling asleep along the way. She had advised me that some passengers, especially around the diamond town of Kimberley, don't have ubuntu and steal other people's luggage when getting off the train. She had experienced this misfortune on her way home to Zimbabwe via Johannesburg.

We passed the Klerksdorp station at about nine in the morning and, as I stood up to stretch, my stomach started to rumble, from hunger, I suspected.

Inside the plastic bag that I had hidden under my seat there was some left-over chicken from KFC. I could have eaten it, but as soon as I tried to open my bag the woman next to me stared at me with nightmarish suspicion. It was as if I were one of those uncivilised bastards she had always warned her daughters not to dare go out on a date with. So I left it in the bag under my seat.

After the train had passed Klerksdorp Station, I decided to go and brush my teeth in the toilet. As I walked down the aisle, with my toothbrush in my hand, I felt my cellphone vibrating inside my Nike sweatpants. The small screen on it registered *Mama*. A shiver ran through me as I answered the phone.

"Hi, Mama . . ."

"Hey, my laaitie, it's your uncle talking on your Mama's cell here. Where are you now?" It was Uncle Nyawana at the other end. "Your ouledi said I should find out."

"Sure, Uncle. We are between Klerksdorp and Potchefstroom and we should be arriving at Park Station around one this afternoon. It's almost an hour behind schedule," I shouted over the noise of the train.

"Sharp, Advo. I'm sure you came with nice things from Cape Town for your uncle. Don't forget my J&B whisky that you promised. A belofte is a belofte, my laaitie."

"Ah . . . Uncle, I only have a UCT T-shirt for you. It's from our law school and has the university logo on it," I struggled, trying to describe the T-shirt. "I'm sure you'll love it, Uncle."

"That sounds nice, my Advo, but I still want my whisky that you promised," he insisted. "Don't worry if you forgot to buy for me in Cape Town, there are lots of bottle stores where we can buy. There are the Lagos and Kinshasa bottle stores in Hillbrow that operate twenty-four hours a day. There is also a nice new bottle store here next to Park Station called Dakar. Or, if you like, we can go to Zak Zak in Diepkloof. That's the cheapest place in the whole of Jozi."

"That's fine, Uncle. We'll see when I get there."

"Good, my laaitie. I'm sure you got an A in your law school report. I know that you're slim."

"We'll talk about that, Uncle. My battery is low and my cell can cut out at any time."

"Sharp, Advo. We'll be waiting for you at Park Station."

My thoughts raced as the feeling of failure and guilt seized me for the first time that morning.

Ever since I had started doing law at the University of Cape Town, my uncle had stopped calling me by my real name, which is Bafana, and started calling me Advo, short for advocate.

Mama also had her expectations. According to her, 1999 was my final year at university and, the following year, I would be starting work as an advocate. Her simple calculation was that a law degree only takes four years to complete, hence I was already doing my final year. She had completely ruled out the possibility that I might fail, which I'm afraid is exactly what had happened.

I'm not sure if this denial by Mama was due to her limited Western education or her excitement. She had left school in standard seven because she'd fallen pregnant with me, but her ambition, as she always told me, had been to become a lawyer. Ever since I started doing law she had boasted to her friend sis Zinhle that I was going to be the youngest advocate to come out of Chi.

I negotiated my way to the next carriage in search of a toilet with a sink. The door to the first one read *Engaged* and I waited outside, looking at the fields through the window.

A few seconds later a lady came out and I went in and locked the door behind me, and started brushing my teeth. I clearly recalled the morning when everything had fallen apart. The morning I went to check the provisional results that were posted on the notice board of the law school. It's not that I'd expected much, but I couldn't believe my eyes when I realised that I had failed everything except for Criminal Law.

TWO
Tuesday, November 23

The concourse of Johannesburg Park Station was busy as always that Tuesday afternoon, but as I emerged from the stairs that led down to platform 15 I couldn't help but see Uncle Nyawana, next to the Greyhound bus counter, flashing his dirty teeth at me. Standing next to him were three people, but I only recognised Dilika and Pelepele, his childhood friends.

Dilika had been my teacher at Progress High School. He couldn't seem to bring himself to begin a sentence without saying "read my lips", a phrase that had quickly become his nickname.

PP was a notorious carjacker in Soweto and his name alone carried terror in the township. His neck and both his arms were covered with grotesque tattoos of a praying mantis, a lion and a gun. He got them during his time in Sun City. He once served a seven-year stretch there and he always boasted that he was the leader of the feared prison gang the 26s. His story convinced a lot of people in the township as he had some big marks or scars on his cheeks, like awkward birthmarks, and he never told anyone how he got them.

As soon as he saw me, my uncle tucked his wooden crutches under his arms and limped towards me with a smile.

"I'm glad you finally arrived, my Advo. Good to see you, and welcome to Jozi maboneng, the place of lights," he said, trying to hug me.

He smelled of a combination of sweat, booze and cigarettes.

"Look at you!" my uncle continued excitedly, "the Mother City has bathed you. You have gained complexion by spending all that time with the ngamlas and dushis. Yeah, you look handsome, my laaitie. All the girls ekasi will be yours."

After twenty-seven gruelling hours trapped inside the crammed third-class carriage of the Shosholoza Meyl, I was exhausted and couldn't say anything. All I could do was smile.

"Come on, meet my bra's," he pointed at his friends with his left crutch. "You know PP and Dilika already, but meet Zero here," he said, pointing at the third guy with widely spaced teeth. "He lives in our back yard. He has erected a zozo there. It's been about three months now. He's a very nice guy."

I immediately dropped one of my bags to shake the damp hand that Zero extended towards me. He wore a traditional Rolex.

"Nice meeting you, Zero," I said, shaking hands with him. His squeeze was very hard, as if he were punishing me for something I had done wrong.

"We've been waiting for you since eleven, Advo," started PP, as we walked to the parking lot along Rissik Street, "and for that you owe us a bottle of J&B."

Very few people remembered or knew PP's real name. I didn't know it either, but it was easy to pick him out of a crowd because of the way he walked. Because of his gout, he stuck his chest out as if it were an arse and walked slowly without his heels touching the ground.

"Read my lips! That's right, PP," added Dilika unnecessarily, "we should be attending a stokvel party at Ndofaya. Advo must buy us ugologo so that we can get there already tipsy."

"Hey, madoda! I told you that my laaitie was a student at the Uni-

12

versity of Cape Town, and not working there. Perhaps we can ask him for a case of J&B next year when he is already the biggest advocate in Msawawa," said Uncle Nyawana protectively.

"Hey, bra Nyawana, read my lips! You must not underestimate the financial power of the students. They have big money from their bursaries and the National Student Financial Aid Scheme," said Dilika with confidence. "When I was a student at Soweto College, there in Pimville in the early eighties, I used to save a lot of money from my Council of Churches bursary. Besides, Advo was my student at Progress High School and he has to pay me because I'm his good ex-thiza who taught him until he got a university exemption. If it wasn't for me, he would have been isibotho, drinking mbamba, or a tsotsi, robbing people here ekasi."

To stop them from arguing I bought a bottle of J&B whisky at the Dakar bottle store next to the parking lot.

* * *

As soon as Zero inserted the key into the ignition of PP's BMW, "Shibobo" by TKZee blasted out from the giant speakers in the boot of the car. As the BMW sped away in the direction of Soweto, my uncle immediately opened the whisky bottle, poured a tot into the cap and swallowed.

"Ahhhh!" Uncle Nyawana opened his mouth wide and looked at the roof of the car as if to allow fresh air into his lungs. "One nine nine nine was a bit of a rough year, Advo, but this coming year of two gees belongs to us, me and you, Advo," he whispered into my ear. His eyes were bloodshot. "We'll be fucking rich. You'll be an advocate and together we'll sue Transnet for my lost leg, my laaitie.

I'm telling you that we'll win the case, as it was all because of their negligence that I lost it. I tell you, we'll be rich, my Advo. Our days as part of the poor walking class of Mzansi will soon be over. We're about to join the driving class, with stomachs made large by the Black Economic Empowerment. Yeah, we'll be fucking rich. Stinking rich, Advo," he repeated over and over again, as if the topic had somehow become trapped in his brain.

"I think so too, Uncle," I said, without meaning it.

"Yeah. We'll buy all the houses in our street and put up boom gates, like they do in the northern suburbs, so the thieves can fuck off," he said, pointing randomly at the mine dump along the M1 South freeway. "But, no," he corrected himself, "I'll buy you a house in the posh suburb of Houghton because ngiyak'ncanywa, ntwana. I love you, my laaitie, and I want you to be Mandela's neighbour and own a mansion with very high walls like all the rich people do. Then you can go around your house naked and your neighbours won't complain or think you're mad, like they would in the township, because they won't be able to see you. We'll also join the cigar club and all Mandela's nieces will fight over you because you'll be stinking rich. You'll be the manager of my businesses and when I die you'll take over, my Advo. We'll buy a funeral parlour and make huge profits from the tenders we'll get from the Department of Aids because people in Msawawa die of those worms every day."

Everyone in the car laughed at my uncle's dreams, but Zero's laughter was derisive.

"If you're black and you failed to get rich in the first year of our democracy, when Tata Mandela came to power, you must forget it, my bra," said Zero. "The gravy train has already passed you by and, like me, you'll live in poverty until your beard turns grey. The bridge between the stinking rich and the poor has been demolished. That is the harsh reality of our democracy."

"Don't listen to him, Advo. He wants you to lose hope. There are opportunities waiting for us in the township," said PP, twisting his neck so that he could look in my direction. I was sitting with my uncle and Dilika in the back seat.

My uncle refilled the whisky cap and passed it over to Zero who was driving. My eyes kept shutting because I was tired, but no one seemed to notice as they were enjoying their whisky.

Dilika pulled my arm so that I could give him my attention.

"Read my lips, Advo, I'm glad that you have finished your law degree. Congratulations!"

"Thanks," I said, tiredly.

"Good! But I want you to advise me on something very serious tomorrow, Advo. It concerns your law. I went to see this majiyane in town and he tells me that I have to pay him four clipa as a consultation fee. Bloody lawyer!" Dilika clicked his tongue in manufactured anger. "I wonder where he thinks I'll raise four hundred bucks, because that's huge zak. Read my lips, Advo, the cost of living has seriously become higher after these tears of apartheid. We teachers are still paid peanuts by our own black ANC government. That's why I can't even afford proper shoes," he said, pointing at his izimbatata sandals. They were handmade from car tyres.

"Hey, my bra," interrupted PP from the passenger seat, where he was smoking a cigarette. "Don't say 'we teachers' because you were fired in August, remember? You're unemployed just like me. You hear that? You and I are both abomahlalela."

Dilika made no effort to defend himself. Instead, he creased his forehead and drank a tot of whisky straight from the bottle as Zero was still holding the cap.

"Arggh, bleksem! Don't worry, nkalakatha, you'll work again," said Uncle Nyawana in a consolatory voice. "Advo will sort that one out for free when he becomes an advocate next year. Is that not so, my laaitie?" asked Uncle Nyawana, but he wasn't expecting an answer from me.

"You're right. That must be his first test as an advocate," said Zero.

Everyone in the township knew Dilika had been dismissed from his teaching job because of his drinking problem. It had all started when I was at home during the winter break in June. Due to his laziness he'd asked me and two of his students that he had chosen from his standard ten class, to help him mark both his standard eight and nine mid-year biology exam scripts. Dilika had promised us a dozen ngudus if we finished the job in time.

The deal was concluded in a shebeen that we called The White House. Some of the scripts got lost in the tavern, but Dilika gave marks to the students nonetheless. This only became a problem when marks had been allocated, by mistake, to a student who had passed away before the exams were even written.

When the private investigators came to Dilika's house, he was drunk and failed to provide an explanation why marks had been given to students whose papers hadn't been marked, including the student that had passed away.

Dilika blamed his misfortune on the students he had selected from his class to help me mark the papers. He believed that since he hadn't paid them for the job they might have alerted the authorities.

Although I had also not been paid for the job, I escaped the blame because I was still in Cape Town when the investigations started.

As the BMW passed the new Gold Reef Casino, PP turned and looked at my uncle. "My bra, your mshana is fucking gifted upstairs," he called out loudly, while drunkenly knocking his own head. "Yes, your nephew's upstairs is sharp as a razor."

"He inherited it from me," said Uncle Nyawana. "Remember, I got position one in our standard two class esgele. It was 1971. There were no computers then, only typewriters."

"Read my lips, my bra! I think you're suffering from what intelligent whites call false memory syndrome, you've never been esgele," teased Dilika. "How could this brilliant young man, who has conquered UCT, the great white man's institution, be like you? If there is a person amongst us that should share his success, it's me. I was his teacher."

Dilika was right about my uncle. He had dropped out of school before I was even born. He had sworn to everyone at home that he would never work for white people and therefore there was no reason for him to be educated, but in actual fact we all knew that he was just too lazy to look for a real job.

"Don't listen to Dilika, my Advo!" Uncle Nyawana said, smiling. "Let me tell you a secret. In our time we were only educated to speak Kaffirkaans. That's the reason I was at the forefront of the 1976 Soweto uprising with Tsietsi Mashinini and others."

We all laughed, but PP's deep-throated laughter drowned everybody else's. We knew that my uncle wasn't telling the truth. I guess he was probably out in the township robbing people when the uprising occurred.

"Read my lips, these kids of today are lucky," interrupted Dilika. "Just look at Advo! Young as he is, he's already going to be an advocate."

A wide smile spread to every corner of my uncle's light-skinned face.

We were now in Chi and Zero turned into our street. We passed the Tsakani meat market which, as usual, was crowded with people roasting their meat, washing their expensive cars and drinking alcohol. From the open window of the BMW I could smell the appetising scent of braai in the air.

Next to the meat market was a beautiful pink house that, some five months earlier, had been an ordinary four-roomed township house belonging to a woman we called maMshangaan. It had been extended while I'd been away, and in addition to the high walls and the paved driveway, the house also had a satellite dish on its tiled roof. I concluded, without asking my uncle, that the owner had become a serious businesswoman, who no longer sold smiley and amanqina.

My uncle's dog, Verwoerd, was sleeping under the apricot tree as the BMW entered our small, dusty driveway. Uncle Nyawana got out of the car first and immediately the dog jumped towards him and nuzzled his hand. But Verwoerd wasn't impressed by my presence. As soon as I climbed out of the car to off-load my luggage, he gazed at me once with his jewelled eyes, then wrinkled his black lips up to show his fangs before he started barking.

"Hey, voetsek, Verwoerd! Uyabandlulula! You discriminate! This is my laaitie, you no longer remember him?" my uncle said, trying to silence his dog.

18

THREE
Wednesday, November 24, Soweto

I was still in my boxers, the first cigarette of the morning between my fingers, when I heard someone approaching the house. I knew that it was Mama because she walked very slowly with a heavy tread. I hadn't expected her to visit us so early in the morning as a few months earlier she had moved in with her lover, Uncle Thulani, in Naturena. In fact, she was three-and-a-half months pregnant with his child.

When I heard Mama's keys jingling at the door, I immediately pressed the burning tip of my cigarette with my fingers to extinguish it. Only my uncle suspected that I smoked and I didn't want Mama to find out.

"Hau, hau, hau! Now that I live in Naturena, Jabu has turned this house into a breeding ground for cockroaches," Mama protested loudly, using Uncle Nyawana's real name. "Sies, man!" she said to herself. "Where are the men of this house? Is anybody home?"

I didn't answer. I could hear some kwaito coming from inside my uncle's room and I thought that he would answer, but he didn't. I guess he was still in the toilet outside.

My uncle would lock himself inside the toilet for about an hour every morning. Inside he performed a strange ritual which involved syringing himself with warm water mixed with Jeyes Fluid. He was convinced that by doing his ukupeyta he would clear his mind and be able to focus on his business as a fruit-and-vegetable vendor at the back of our house. He also believed that ukupeyta and ukuphalaza were the only ways to get rid of bad luck and township witch-craft. In a way I regretted ignoring his advice. Maybe I would have passed my law exams if I had listened to him, but, unfortunately, I just found his morning practice of ukupeyta and ukuphalaza very funny as he would repeatedly curse every time he drove the hollow needle into his arse.

In the kitchen I heard plastic bags rustling and then, a few seconds later, Mama burst into a personal rendition of a kwaito song by Bongo Muffin that was coming from my uncle's radio.

Thathi's sgubu usfak'ezozweni.	(Take the drum and put it in the shack.)
Ufak'amspeks uzobuzwa . . .	(Put on your glasses and you'll feel . . .)
Ubumnandi obulapho.	(The joy that is there.)

I laughed inside my room as I imagined the meaning of the song and my overweight mother singing it. She paused and called my name again.

"Bafana! Are you still in bed in there, my son?" she shouted.

"I'm here, Mama."

"I haven't seen you for ages. Wake up and come have breakfast with me while we chat. I want you to tell me everything about Cape Town, and I mean, everything. I bought you a newspaper as well. They're looking for a legal advisor in this advert."

"I'm coming, Mama."

"Sheshisa! Hurry up! I'm dying to see how my boy looks. Five months is a very long time for a mother not to see her son. And Yuri's here too."

20

Yuri was my ten-year-old cousin whose mother, Aunt Thandi, had died of Aids-related diseases at the age of twenty-seven. Aunt Thandi was Mama's younger sister. On her death certificate it said that she had died of tuberculosis, chronic diarrhoea and pneumonia.

Two days before she passed away, my sickly Aunt Thandi had called me into her bedroom with a feeble wave of her thin hand and asked me to help her remove a big rock from her chest. She had been coughing badly; coughing up slime and blood.

I still wish I could have helped Aunt Thandi to remove the rock she was talking about, but I didn't see any such thing when I got there. When I tried to tell her about the rock she asked me to help her turn over, but I was afraid of touching her. She was so thin and weak that I was sure that if I touched her, I would catch her disease.

My family had chosen to believe Aunt Thandi's infection was a result of negligence by the hospital. It was said that some time back, before Yuri's birth, Aunt Thandi had been involved in a car accident and had lost a lot of blood. At the hospital she was given a blood transfusion and that was how she had contracted HIV.

"Wow, look at you! I like that complexion," said Mama as soon as I walked into the kitchen, wearing my fur-lined slippers. "Come here and give Mama a big hug."

She squeezed me hard against her enormous pear-shaped breasts as if I had been lost for a decade.

"You look fine too, Mama."

"So, tell me about your university results," she said, as soon as she let go of me. "I know that my boy has done well. I can't wait to see you in a suit with that black gown that lawyers and advocates wear in court!"

21

"Eeee-eh . . ." my reply was slow to come, "that's what I was hoping to discuss with you, Mama."

"What happened? Do you want to take me to the graduation ceremony? I don't mind going to Cape Town with you even though I'm like this . . ." She rubbed her belly. "It would be a great opportunity because I've never been to the Mother City. I was talking about it with Zinhle when we saw a nice dress at Southgate Mall the other day. I wanted to buy it specially for your big day."

"No, Mama. The university has withheld my results because I owe them money," I lied. "So, until I've paid them, they won't give me the results."

"That university is very greedy! How do they think you'll become an advocate without your results, huh?" she asked crossly. "Tell them that you'll settle your debts when you're working as an advocate next year. I'm sure they can give you an extension?"

"I tried that, Mama, but they wouldn't listen to me."

"Ag, shame, my baby! Don't stress . . ." She tried to comfort me by hugging me again. "I'm sure we can make a plan."

I shrugged and looked at Mama.

"But how, Mama?" I asked, my voice devoid of interest. "I owe them R22 000. How can you afford to pay the university?"

"Just leave everything up to Mama, okay? In the meantime you can apply for this job," she said, pointing at the newspaper on the kitchen table.

"No, Mama," I shook my head, "I don't want you to go to the abomashonisa again. You know how those loan sharks are, they'll take all your money if you fail to pay on time."

"Actually, I wasn't even thinking about them."

"Am I missing something here?" I asked as I saw her smile. "Does this mean that the supermarket is paying you well these days?"

"Are you trying to be funny, Bafana?" she asked, the smile vanishing from her face. "What can I do with R21 an hour, huh? You tell me."

"Why don't you join the workers' union, Mama?" I asked.

Mama raised her eyebrows and gave me a sour look. She was sweating a bit above her upper lip.

"Iyhooo! Do you want them to fire me like they did with the others? Ask Zinhle what they did to her before she completed her nursing course. I can't risk that! Where will I get the money to put the food on the table if I join the union, huh? Those rich bastards don't care about us South Africans because of the illegal immigrants. That's why they were so quick to fire Zinhle in the first place, they know it's easy to get these amakwere-kwere and underpay them. No, I've joined a stokvel society and it'll be my turn next month. I think I'll make a good profit. It'll be way too short to pay for your results, but it'll be something."

By that time Yuri had entered the kitchen, followed by my uncle's dog, Verwoerd. Every time that I looked at Yuri, he reminded me of the slow, painful death of his mother.

"Stop that!" Mama shouted at Yuri angrily as he started scratching at his little hand until his skin broke. Then she looked at me and said, "He always does that when he's hungry. I left his food at home in Naturena."

"I don't mind running to the shop and buying him a kota with cheese and a Vienna," I offered.

"No, his sickness requires that I feed him a special diet," said

Mama. "He's only allowed the chicken stew I make with onion, garlic, potatoes, carrots, pumpkin and green beans. I'll have to leave for Naturena now," she said, standing up. "You'll have to make your own breakfast. I'll see you tomorrow morning."

FOUR
Thursday, November 25

The following morning, before she went to work, Mama passed by
our house in Chi again. To my utter astonishment, she asked me
to draft an advert for the sale of our house. At first I thought my
ears were playing elaborate tricks on me, but when she insisted
that I should send the advert to the *Sowetan* newspaper offices in
Industria for publication the following day, I realised she was serious. I was completely against the idea because Uncle Nyawana was
still living in the house and although my elder uncle, Guava, was
in jail for arson and assault, he was still part of our family and it
was his house as well. I thought it was unfair of Mama to decide
to sell the house without speaking to my uncles.

"But Mama, have you discussed this with my uncles?" I asked.

"There's no need to do that now. Besides, both of your uncles
have RDP houses, in Snake Park and Slovoville respectively. It's
only a matter of time before they leave this house for their low-cost
houses."

"What about the family history in this house? I'm sure we're not
that desperate."

"You need your results so that you can start earning a salary for
yourself, don't you, Bafana? This house means nothing to the kind
of money that you'll be earning once you've become an advocate.
You can buy thousands of these houses in just one year," she said,
trying to convince me. "Anyway, all the memories in this place are
bad ones. Both your grandparents died here and your uncle Guava

went to jail straight from this house. There are no good memories here. Just don't tell your uncle about our plan yet."

"Okay, how much shall I advertise it for?"

"What do you think? I mean, there are no improvements; it's still two bedrooms, a dining room, a kitchen and a small yard. The house isn't even plastered."

"But houses are expensive nowadays, Mama."

"Make it forty thousand then."

"Okay, fine, Mama."

As I was talking to Mama in the kitchen I looked out through the dirty window into our small, dusty driveway and saw Priest Mthembu approaching. He lived in the house at the corner of our street and preached nearby at the Roma church. Looking at the black briefcase that he was carrying, I guessed that he was on his way home from his night shift at the Croesus yeast company.

My uncle had just come out from the toilet after doing his morning ritual and was now smoking a zol under the apricot tree. As Priest Mthembu approached, I called out to my uncle.

"A-ye-ye, Uncle! Sek'shubile! Danger! The priest is here," I warned him, expecting him to put out the zol that he was smoking.

"Yeah, Bafana is right. What will the priest say when he sees you smoking dagga, huh Jabu?" said Mama. "He'll probably think that we don't have any respect in this house."

"Priest Mthembu knows very well that I don't respect him. He once said to my face that I'm a heathen and will not go to heaven," responded my uncle.

By a stroke of luck, Priest Mthembu didn't hear my uncle as he had seen someone he knew and had stopped to greet him.

26

"And I stopped attending his evangel when he started preaching that Jesus was not the son of Mary and Joseph, but the son of God and the Holy Spirit," continued my uncle, puffing away at his zol. "We argued a lot about that, Advo," he said, almost in a whisper, "and that's when I stormed out of his church because I can't be taught lies." He threw the remainder of his zol on the ground.

"Shhhhhh, Jabu! He's already here," warned Mama, going into my bedroom where she had left her handbag.

Within seconds Priest Mthembu was knocking at the steel kitchen door.

"Oh my boy, I heard that you had arrived from Cape Town and I thought that I should come and welcome you home," said Priest Mthembu as I opened the door to him.

"Thank you very much, Baba Mfundisi. I was thinking of coming to your house yesterday, but then I thought you would be at work," I lied as he shook my hand.

"I see. Are you coming to church this Sunday?"

"Well, I . . ."

"Sawubona, Baba Mfundisi," said Mama, coming out of the bed-room carrying her handbag. "I'm already late for the train. I'll see you on Sunday."

"Before you leave, let us pray for the unborn child," said Priest Mthembu. "Father," he started as we obediently closed our eyes, "we thank you for your marvellous gift. During this time of waiting, we ask you to protect and nurture the mysterious stirrings of life. May our child come safely into the light of the world. Mother of God, we entrust our child to your loving heart. Ngegama lika Yise neleNdo-dana noMoya Ocwebileyo. In the name of the Father, the Son and the Holy Spirit, Amen!" He made a cross on his chest.

"Amen, Baba Mfundisi! Let me go before the train comes," Mama insisted.

"I'm also not staying. I was just passing by to see Bafana here and to remind him to come to church on Sunday. The choir misses him." He turned to Uncle Nyawana who had just come through the kitchen door and asked, "You're coming along, Jabu, aren't you?"

It was the first time that I had ever heard someone from outside my family use my uncle's real name. Ever since he had lost his leg in the accident people had called him uNyawana. Although it's an uncomplimentary nickname, my uncle never complained.

"No, church and I don't mix and you know that, Baba Mfundisi," said Uncle Nyawana, going into his bedroom.

"I'm not losing hope, Jabu," responded Priest Mthembu, pointing after my uncle. "You must know that God loves you."

* * *

My uncle only came out of his room when Priest Mthembu had left for his own house. By then Mama had also left for work.

"Hola, Uncle, it seems you don't believe in Jesus," I said.

"It's not a question of believing in God or Jesus, my laaitie. It's whether They believe what is important to me. I might not be educated like you, but I'm not an idiot. How can I believe in a man who was convinced that His own mother, Mary, was a virgin? Just look at it, Advo! She carried Him for nine full pregnant and painful months, but Jesus still denied that Mary was His own mother."

"But I already promised Priest Mthembu that we're coming to his church together this Sunday," I teased. "Is that the only reason you won't come with me?"

"I grew up respecting my parents, Advo," he said. "Even though my father was a drunk, I still respected him. Jesus never did that to His parents. He disowned them."

I laughed out loud while my uncle limped to his room and came out with a glass full of whisky. He stopped and took a sip before belching loudly.

"Ahhhhh! This is my Garden of Eden. I tell you, Advo, if Jesus and God were not dead, They would come down from heaven to have a sip with me. This would make Them forget Their Christian confusion." He kissed his glass and laughed at his own joke.

"But, Uncle, we must be thankful for the life that God gave us," I said.

"Life! Come on, Advo," shouted my uncle. "I'm not going to waste my time bribing God with prayers. Whatever I say to Him, He won't bring back the leg that I lost twelve years ago."

"Let's leave God out of this, Uncle," I said, trying to change the topic.

"To tell you the truth, Advo, it was not a mistake or oversight that I lost my leg. God did it deliberately to punish me because I was a tsotsi." He pointed at his stump. "It was part of His plan that I should be a cripple from the age of twenty-nine."

Memories of the day of his accident started to flood into my mind. I recalled coming home from school with my sister, Nina, and hearing that my uncle was in hospital, but I wanted him to tell me more about it.

"What happened on the day you lost your leg, Uncle?" I asked.

"It's a long story, Advo. Let's not even go there."

"But I want to know, Uncle," I insisted.

"Okay, okay, I'm only telling you this on condition that the first thing you do as an advocate next year is to sue Transnet for millions."

Silence fell for a while as my uncle took another sip from his glass.

"Well, it happened a very long time ago, in 1987. Let me see, how old were you then?" He scratched his head. "I think you were about four or five years old, a real pikinini. You were still sucking Rea's breasts."

"No, Uncle, I was nine in 1987," I corrected him.

"Yeah, but I remember the popular beer was Lion Lager then."

"Okay, fine with Lion Lager and my age now, Uncle. I want to know what happened to your leg," I said, interrupting his thoughts. "Tell me everything."

"All right then. It happened on my way home from Jozi. I was with PP and we were empty-handed. Then inside the garo I saw this woman sitting alone at the far end of the coach. Some smokser came in selling ice cream and the woman opened her purse for some money. Inside it . . . Advo, phew!" He whistled. "There were banknotes this thick." He demonstrated, using his forefinger and thumb. "PP saw her as well."

"So you and PP have always been bra's and tsotsis?"

"We've been friends for a very long time, since we were pikininis, my laaitie. We dropped out of school at the same time because isgele was just not meant for us. It was meant for people like Dilika."

"So what happened?"

"Oh, I think the woman was going to Vreega with the train, so I looked around and aimed at her purse. As the garo picked up speed away from the station, PP was already at the sliding door blocking it with his body so that it didn't close. We were good at sparapara and that's why we were planning to come out with the purse while the train was still moving, but as I stepped out, holding the purse, I tripped and fell."

My uncle suddenly stopped his narration. His sausage-like fingers were nursing the whisky glass on his palm. There was an expression of bitterness on his face.

"I'm telling you this because I'm glad ugelezile. You're educated. You're going to be an advocate next year and not a tsotsi like most boys here in Chi."

"Thank you, Uncle."

"I want us to sue Transnet for my lost leg. Yeah, we must sue them," he repeated.

"On what grounds are we going to sue them, Uncle?" I asked.

"You know what, Advo? Some people say that I was pushed off the train by a security guard who worked for Transnet. They say that he was inside the train and heard the woman's cry for help."

"Do you have enough evidence for that, Uncle? I mean, did you see him push you?"

"My witness is PP. He says that he saw the guy push me, but I don't remember anything. All I know is that my leg was amputated below the knee three days later."

FIVE
Tuesday, November 30

Five days after I had placed the advertisement for the sale of our Chi house with the *Sowetan* newspaper, an old man walked up our dusty driveway. He stopped and looked up at our house number that was scrawled on the unplastered brick wall outside the front door. He looked at least seventy, or maybe a bit more; both his hair and beard were grey and he was wearing an old brown suit with black shoes. Suddenly he seemed to come to some kind of a decision and knocked at the kitchen door.

I saw Mama open the door, which was still the original steel one that made a loud bang when you opened or closed it, but I kept staring at the old man. I had never known my father, or my paternal grandfather, and I had long ago accepted the fact that I was the product of a man who didn't care that I existed and a woman who hid the truth from me all the time. I didn't miss the man who ran away without seeing the fruits of his handsome labour, but for some reason I was hoping that Mama was going to announce the old man as my grandfather.

By the time I got to the kitchen the old man was already sitting on one of the plastic chairs while Mama rested on one of the others with a puzzled look on her face. The two of them were examining each other with great curiosity.

"My name is John Sekoto," the old man introduced himself to Mama. "I used to live in this house in the early seventies, before I leased it out to Mr Kuzwayo in 1974."

"Sawubona, mkhulu," Mama greeted the old man, "I'm the late Kuzwayo's daughter and my name is Rea."

"I see. Are you Nandi's daughter?"

"Yebo, mkhulu."

"You look more like your mother. You were still young when I was transferred to the Welkom mines."

Mama smiled.

"You see, I was just discharged from the Weskoppies Mental Hospital in Pretoria. I had been there for almost two decades and right now I don't have a place to stay. I read in the *Sowetan* newspaper that this house was up for sale and I thought that I should come here and discuss some issues with you."

"Oh, you're right. It's been a month now and we're waiting for a potential buyer," Mama lied.

The old man nodded.

"My two brothers have got their new RDP houses from the ANC government in Snake Park and Slovoville and now there's nobody to live here. We've got another house in Naturena," Mama boasted, "and that's the reason we're selling this one. You're the third person to respond to the advert since we placed it in the newspaper again last week. Do you want to have a look around while I make you some coffee or tea?"

"Actually, I don't think you understand the reason I'm here," said the old man, looking Mama straight in the face. "What I mean to say is that this is my house and you can't sell it. In fact, I would like to reoccupy it and I thought that I should give you two months' notice."

I was surprised at the old man's claim and I listened wide-eyed.

"What's that supposed to mean, huh?" Mama finally managed to say, staring viciously at him. "That this is your house?"

"Like I said, I'm afraid it's the truth," the old man responded with calmness in his voice.

Mama clicked her tongue and shook her head as if she had just woken up from a nightmare.

"We've lived in this house for our whole lives and now, all of a sudden, somebody from a mental hospital claims it's his? No way! Never! What proof have you got to show that this is your house, huh?" she said, raising her voice.

"Well, I have several photos of me and my family, as well as some papers," said the old man.

Silence fell while the old man took out six faded black-and-white pictures from his pocket and, uncomfortably, pushed them across the table towards Mama. I approached the table to have a better look at them. The pictures were almost identical. In each one of them he had posed with three other people, but before he even began to tell us about the people in the pictures, I had guessed that they were his wife and two sons. The sons looked like they were aged between two and four when the photo was taken. In the background of each picture was a number that was scrawled in white paint on the wall of a house. It appeared on the brick wall next to the steel door and it read 9183. That was our house number. The very same house that Mama was selling so that she could pay for my nonexistent university results.

Mama looked away.

"That's my wife there," said the old man, pointing at the woman in the photograph that Mama was still holding. "She used to be a great friend of Nandi, your mother," he continued in a nostalgic tone of a voice. "Ah, those days . . ."

"And where is she now?" Mama asked, as if she had suddenly remembered something about the woman.

"I last saw her in 1979, immediately before I was committed to Weskoppies."

The old man looked at the asbestos roof of our house and smiled, and at that moment, I was convinced that he was still mad. Mama watched him as well, not moving.

"Oh, I was looking at that hole up there." The old man pointed at the roof of the house. "It happened in 1972, during the rent boycott," he continued. "The police were shooting all over the township."

Mama appeared uninterested in what the old man was saying. She looked very tired and annoyed, but, indeed, there was a hole where he was pointing to and the roof always leaked slightly from there when it rained.

"And where are your children?" Mama asked, her expressionless eyes meeting those of the old man.

"The older one, Tumi, died in 1978 when I was in Welkom and the other one, Pule, I don't know where he is. I'm still looking for him and his mother. I heard that they're somewhere here in Jo'burg."

Mama frowned before she fired another question at him.

"So, what other proof do you have to support your claim that this is your house, huh? I mean, where is your title deed for this house?"

The old man searched his pocket again and came out with a very old, dog-eared document that looked like a passport, only bigger. He handed it to Mama. As I moved closer to see what was written

in it, I saw the words *Residential Permit Holder* written on the outside in black. Inside there was a black-and-white photograph of the
old man when he was still middle-aged. There were also finger-
prints, the old man's date of birth (which happened to be 1928), his
race, sex, names of his previous employers and their addresses,
how long he had been employed there and so forth. In one section
the pages were stamped in red, stating *Permission Request Denied*
or *Permission Request Granted*.

Mama turned to the next page which was headed *Lawful Dependants*. Three dependants as well as their ages were mentioned. The
old man's wife was called Tseli and she had been born in 1941.
Their son Tumi was born in 1960 and the other one, Pule, was
born in 1963. The document was stamped with the words *Urban
Dwellers*. There were also two pink cards with the children's names
on them and they bore the official stamps of the primary schools
they had been attending. In the permit I also saw our house number again: 9183, Chiawelo Section Two, Soweto.

His papers looked genuine although they were old.

"Is this what you call a title deed, huh?" Mama asked with an
expression of pure scorn on her face.

"Yes, that's it," the old man replied, but at that moment Uncle
Nyawana came limping through the door carrying his syringe in
his hand.

"Jabu, listen to this old man here. He says he has come to occupy this house because it's his and he leased it out to our parents
in seventy-something. He shows us these old papers and a dompas,
and expects us to believe him," she said contemptuously.

"He's mad," my uncle declared, tapping at the side of his own head with his finger. "I told him a month ago already, when he was here before, that we have the title deed for this house. I forgot to tell you about him because I didn't think it was important. He's mentally disturbed."

"I have a title deed in my room and it says the house belongs to my father, Sbusiso Kuzwayo," said Mama. "Do you hear me? Sbusiso Kuzwayo, my father," she repeated. "Go fetch the title deed, Bafana, it's in the suitcase in the wardrobe."

Within seconds I was back with the title deed. Mama was right, the house belonged to Mr Sibusiso Kuzwayo, my late grandfather, who passed away in 1992. According to the document, the title right of the former council house was bestowed on him on the 10th of June in 1989 at the cost of R1 300. There was no indication in the document that the house had once belonged to some John Sekoto. Mama showed the document to the old man with confidence.

"Ahhh, I sensed this was going to happen," said the old man, flushing with rage. "I knew it. Your father arranged that title deed when he heard I had been committed to Weskoppies."

"That's not important now, is it?" interrupted my uncle. "It's your problem if you think that my father robbed you of this house. Don't make your problem ours. My father knew you were mad, but this house legally belongs to the Kuzwayo family, so you must fuck off."

The humiliation on the old man's dark face was plain, but my doubts about his claim had started to abandon me. I believed him. When I looked into his eyes again I felt pity for him and, in that moment, I began to dislike my uncle and Mama's attitude towards him. The manner in which they talked to him was disrespectful and Mama had raised me to always be respectful to the elders.

"But it's my house. You have no right," insisted the old man.

"Uyabhema yini, mkhulu?" asked my uncle in a condescending tone. "I think you must have smoked a lot of zol because you don't listen! I told you not to come here again with your bullshit stories. It seems you didn't take me seriously then?" he said, his tone full of manufactured anger.

The old man didn't answer, but he looked intimidated.

"Now, let me be fair with you, madala, because I hate bullshit! I tell you for the last time," Uncle Nyawana shouted impatiently, as if he had reached the limit of his tolerance with the old man, "if you want to know what the devil looks like, just come here again and I'll show you. Do you hear me, madala? I'll cut your crazy head off with that axe over there and feed it to my dog, Verwoerd."

The old man stood up, but his eyes were darting into the four corners of our kitchen.

"But I want my house back. I'm giving you two months' notice," he insisted nervously. "If I have to go to the highest court in the land to get back what rightfully belongs to me, I will," he said, standing at the door. "I can't allow somebody to be the proud owner of my house. The umbilical cords of my two sons are buried in this yard."

"Who do you think you are to come here with your old useless papers and claim this house is yours, huh?" Mama demanded angrily. "Hamba! Go away!"

I felt very sorry for the old man as he walked out of our house with the submissiveness of a man who had just lost a fight. I watched him turning his head to look at both ends of the street as soon as he was at the end of the yard. It was as if he were debating with himself which way to go.

SIX
Wednesday, December 1

The following day I found myself sitting behind our family house next to Uncle Nyawana's fruit-and-vegetable stall. In his left hand, my uncle was holding what he called his dream notebook, which he used to play fah-fee. Verwoerd was curled at my uncle's feet with one eye open, watching me. I was sitting on an empty beer crate that was turned upside down. A pair of shears were on the ground in front of me as I'd been busy trimming the lawn since eight that morning. I was just about to wipe away the sweat that was streaming down my face when my cellphone started to ring and the name *Mama* appeared on the small screen.

"Hi, Mama."

"Hello, baby, how are you this morning?"

"I'm fine, Mama."

"Listen, I'm calling to ask you for a favour. I can see that your uncle is not concerned about it, but I am. I want you to go to the local Housing Department." She paused.

"Where's that?" I asked.

"I don't know exactly, but I think it's somewhere in Jo'burg city centre. I'm sure you'll find it. I want you to go there and make certain that we are the rightful owners of the house."

"Okay, Mama. When do you want me to go there?"

"As soon as possible, today or tomorrow at the latest."

"Okay, I'll go tomorrow morning," I said. "It's already late today and the queue there must be very long by now."

"Please do that. I'll see you in the morning . . . Oh, by the way, I saw a job advert in today's *Star*. There is a company that is looking for a legal adviser. That's why we have to get your results as soon as possible. The house must be sold or else you'll lose out on opportunities like this one. Your profession is in high demand, Bafana. I'll come with the newspaper in the morning."

"But, Mama, I think they're looking for experienced people."

"Oh, they only need two years' experience and that's nothing, you meet all the other requirements. Just tell them that you're fresh from one of the country's biggest law schools."

"Okay, Mama. If you come with the advert I'll try to apply," I said hesitantly, afraid to disappoint her.

"All right, baby, but you really must apply for this job. Let me read the benefits to you," she said excitedly. "The salary range is R290 000 to R350 000 per annum. Uh, there is a thirteenth cheque as well and all they want is your LLB degree. That one you have, baby. They also need basic computer literacy and good listening skills, which I'm sure is nothing to you."

"Fine, Mama, I'll try."

I finished talking on my cellphone and put it on the brick next to the lawn. My uncle was standing right behind me, but he seemed to be concentrating on his notebook rather than on the conversation I had just had with Mama.

"So, tell me, Advo, what did you dream about last night?" he asked, scratching out something in his notebook with his pen.

"Let me think, Uncle," I responded, wiping away the sweat that was running down my face with the T-shirt that I was wearing.

"We don't have much time, Advo," he said, his eyes swinging in the direction of maMfundisi's house. "That Chinese man, Liu, is coming in thirty minutes to collect all the bets."

"Okay, give me a minute to remember, Uncle."

"At ten o'clock that Fong Kong will be here."

"All right, that dream is coming now, Uncle."

He looked down at my watch, which he was wearing without my permission. Impatiently, he tucked his crutches under his arms and limped towards the low fence. He put his right hand up to his forehead to shield his eyes from the sun.

At the corner of the street a group of women had gathered and, within seconds, Priest Mthembu's wife, maMfundisi, appeared. Not only was she Priest Mthembu's wife, which is why we called her ma-Mfundisi, but she was also the person who ran the fah-fee game in our part of Chi. I had heard from my uncle that her husband wasn't aware that she was involved in fah-fee. The money bags that she was carrying were to be given to Liu.

Upon seeing maMfundisi, my uncle shouted, "I'm on my way, maMfundisi! Please wait for my bet!"

My uncle gave me an impatient stare as if he had just found a fresh reason to be angry with me.

"Please hurry, Advo! Liu will be here any moment now."

"Okay, Uncle, it was a bad dream that I had last night and I'm not sure if I should tell you about it."

"That's fine, my laaitie, every dream has a number and a meaning in this game."

"All right, Uncle . . ."

"Go on, I'm listening."

"Mama caught me smoking a cigarette and scolded me."

"Good! That's a very good dream, my Advo," said my uncle, barely concealing his delight. "When someone scolds you, the number to play is twenty-four."

He wrote down the number in his notebook in his deformed, semi-literate handwriting.

"And then what happened?"

"Well, she called me a pig and broke my cigarette into pieces."

"Aha! She called you a pig?" he asked, laughing. "Did she really say that?"

"Yes, she did, in my dream, of course."

He nodded slowly in approval.

"Okay, a pig is number eight. This is why I like you, Advo. Ever since you came back here from Cape Town I'm a lucky person."

I smiled while my uncle held forth on his favourite subject.

"My dreams are always bad for this game, Advo," he said. "I tell you, just a week before you came back I dreamt of my dog Verwoerd's penis. I played thirty-six, because a penis is that number in fah-fee, and I lost all my money."

"Ha, ha, ha," I laughed, "is that right?"

My uncle smiled and slapped my back tenderly.

"That's the truth, my laaitie. Your dreams are real because you're very educated."

My uncle was still scribbling some numbers on a piece of paper when a white four-wheel drive Toyota van passed stealthily along our street. Inside the bulletproof van were two Chinese guys wearing panama hats.

The car stopped in the middle of the street next to maMfundisi's house where the group of women had gathered. Uncle Nyawana immediately gave me a piece of paper with the numbers on it, as well as R48.

"Look, Advo!" he said, spitting on the ground playfully. "If you come back before this saliva dries up, I'll buy you four ngudus of Hansa Pilsner."

With my uncle's promise on my mind I ran immediately towards maMfundisi's house, passing some kids that were playing hop-scotch on the street. At the gate of her house I gave maMfundisi the bet and watched as she approached the car. The window was rolled down and I saw a hand receiving four bags of money.

When I got back to our house, my uncle was sitting on the beer crate and a woman was sitting on the lawn next to him.

"The millennium is just around the corner," the woman was say-ing to my uncle, "so I have come here to make peace with you. Priest Mthembu told us that those who sin by hating others are not going to see the Kingdom of God."

"Good! I forgive you," said my uncle, as if he had been the wronged party, "and where is Mbuso?"

"He's at work. He finally got a job. But he'll also come to make peace with you because it's not a good thing to hate each other. He understands that it was a mistake that you and your friends beat him so badly."

They shook hands and the woman left. My uncle limped towards his room with his empty glass in his hand. He came back a few minutes later with the glass full of whisky.

"What was that all about, Uncle? Is she your girlfriend?" I joked.

"Girlfriend? Hell no, she's too old for me, Advo. She's the mother of that guy Mbuso, the one who was staying here until June."

"You mean that guy who was staying where Zero's zozo is now? I heard that you knocked his teeth out after he failed to pay the rent in time?"

"Exactly. The same guy who made us sleep in a prison cell for a week in winter. I tell you that if it was not for bra PP, who bribed the police officials with two straights of KWV brandy, we would still be in jail now. Money can really talk in this country, Advo. I've seen it."

"But why did you beat him up? You should have simply told him to leave."

"You don't understand, Advo. It wasn't that simple. You see that hosepipe in the toolbox behind the toilet?"

"Yes. What about it?"

"That guy came back in the evening, just after I'd told him to pack and go. I was out drinking at The White House with PP and Dilika, but when I came back at midnight my room was flooded. My bed, my clothes and everything was all wet. And, imagine, it was a very cold winter."

"How did you know that it was him?"

"He was the only suspect, Advo. Who else could it have been, huh?"

"Maybe it was one of your old grudges, Uncle. I mean, you have no evidence it was him?"

"I knew it was him, Advo. He'd said during the day that he'd get me for throwing him out. The following morning I went to his home with PP and Dilika and we beat the shit out of him until he confessed."

I shook my head in disapproval, but I still wanted to hear more.

"And that old man who came to the house yesterday and claimed it was his, who's he?" I asked.

"Oh, that happened when your grandfather, my father, was still working at the city council. That man, my taima, was a real tsotsi. Many people lost their houses because of him. You see here, opposite, the Jobe's place, where we ask for ice cubes every day, neh?"

"Yes, what about it?"

"They got that house through my taima. Some old man and his wife used to live there and they had no children. When they died in '91, my father organised that the house be registered to the Jobe family. I think he was screwing Jobe's wife . . ."

"So what's going to happen about the old man's claim?"

"He can go to the city council to check if he wants, but there's nothing he can do because the original title deed is still in our family's name. You saw that, didn't you, Advo?"

I nodded.

SEVEN
Thursday, December 2

At eight forty-five the following morning I was already inside a mini-bus taxi on my way to town. Mama had given me R30 for the journey, but I had specifically waited for Zero's taxi as I didn't want to pay the taxi fare to the city.

"You're dressed very smart, Advo," said Zero, as I sat in the front seat next to him.

"Thanks, man," I replied, smiling at his compliment. I was wearing an expensive white Polo T-shirt, a black leather jacket, black suede Carvela shoes and a pair of grey, five-pocketed corduroy pants.

Zero himself was wearing a black T-shirt with Tupac's head printed on it, but the smell that came from his left armpit was an unusually cruel punishment. It was like a rat had decomposed somewhere under his arm and I'm sure I would have suffocated if it were not for the open window on my left. No wonder Mama had nicknamed him magez'epompini.

"Are you going to work this late, Advo?" Zero asked. "PP would kill me if I arrived later than half past five in the morning."

"Yeah, I've got a meeting with a judge in town," I lied.

Just after the Chiawelo clinic, near Senaone, along the Old Potchefstroom Road, I saw a lovely lady pointing her finger to the sky. Her pink T-shirt clearly defined her upper body and she was wearing a pair of white jeans so tight that I don't think she could have bent over to pick something off the ground without them tearing.

Zero stopped the taxi for her to get in and as soon as she opened the door I smelled her strong perfume. It was as if she wore it to get rid of all the bad township smells. As she walked down the almost nonexistent aisle of the taxi with her head bent down to avoid banging it against the roof, her orange G-string was clearly visible.

"Hello, Bunjubunju, my Venus, my goddess of sexual beauty and love," said Zero with a voice that was spiked with desire.

"Hi, Zero," shouted the lady as she sat in the back seat, her face glistening with a smile.

"Mmmmmm! I smelled you even before you left your house. Ohhhh! That perfume, baby, you drive me crazy!" he said, widening his hairy nostrils. "Ahhhh! It smells so gooooood! I feel like eating you like an apple."

Bunju smiled broadly, like a child who had just received an unexpected gift. She seemed to be pleased with Zero's charm, although the sweat ran down his unwashed face like soft porridge boiling over the edge of my uncle's blackened pot.

"Thanks, but you're so scarce these days," she said. "You no longer phone or visit me."

"Ahhhhh, my Bunjubunju! You know that I still love you more than payday, but it's this job. It doesn't give me time to come and see you. I work from Monday to Sunday. There's no holiday if you work for rich people like PP."

The conversation with Bunju stopped as Zero saw some potential commuters. Zero's hand was immediately on the horn as he tried to attract more passengers. He pointed his finger skywards, signalling that he was going to the city, but no one was interested.

"She's the deliciousest of the deliciousest. Did you see her arse,

Advo? She's gifted with the reverse, isn't she?" he said as soon as he was sure no one was interested in his taxi.

"Who are you talking about?" I asked, resisting the urge to look at Bunju.

Zero's eyes darted from me to the rear-view mirror and back to the road. "Come on, man!" he said. "I'm talking about my Bunju. I saw you staring at her arse." He smiled and looked into the rear-view mirror again. "They say you can look, but never touch!"

"Yeah, it's true. She can sue you for sexual harassment if you're not careful nowadays," I said to Zero.

"But you see, Advo, these ladies nowadays have a way of challenging us men. You'll be surprised at what we taxi drivers see in our taxis every day. Some of them don't even bother to wear panties at all. Some of them wear revealing miniskirts just to challenge you, man. That's why Avalon Cemetery is full, it's because these ladies are living advertisements for Aids. I tell you, Advo."

Mama had warned me that Zero and PP had one thing in common and that I should keep away from them as much as possible. She told me that they were notorious for undressing every member of the female species that they saw with their eyes. According to her, they lived in the over-sexualised township world. In Zero and PP's universe, Mama once told me, a man was a man according to the number of ladies he was dating.

"You know what, Advo?" Zero whispered. "Bunju was once my meat and I used to chew her every day."

"And what happened between you two?"

"No, I'm no longer interested in her and I don't care what she does with her pussy now," he said, looking at me.

"But I think she's perfect for you, man."

"Yeah, you're right, she's a perfect pain in the arse," he responded uninterestedly.

"What happened?"

"She thinks that I'm her walking ATM. It's as if I have to pay to have sex with her and, since I left her, she behaves like those motor mechanics that you see in the Midway scrapyards. Yeah, she's always lying on her back for men to screw her for money. She's a puff and pass, man. You can have her if you're curious to know about what's hiding under those panties, but I'm telling you now that those nice curves of hers are dangerous. She's a social worker. Uyagayana. She gives. Don't tell me that you don't know about that?"

"Of course I don't know. I only came back to the township recently. I don't know many people here."

"I think we should spend some time together at The White House this Saturday. You always have your nose buried in a book, Advo, it's not healthy, my bra. You'll go mad. I can hook you up with a nice mntwana."

"I didn't know that it was that simple."

"Siriyasi, I'm telling you, Advo, there's a minimum of five chicks for every dick in Soweto," emphasised Zero.

"Is that so?"

"Siriyasi, Baba. Sure. I already have a new release, man. I got this new chick during a funeral some months back. When I saw her by the graveside that day, I knew she was going to be mine," he said, touching his left breast tenderly to show his love.

"Are you serious? But how did you get her by the graveside, man?" I found myself unable to resist asking him.

Before he could answer, Zero beamed broadly and nodded his head. My question seemed to have excited him and he was smiling as if I had just caught him fondling Miss Universe's breasts in his zozo.

"That's a good question, Advo. A good question indeed," he repeated. "I always do my homework on the beautiful things that appeal to my heart. Even PP knows that he can't compete with me when it comes to beautiful chicks." He slapped his chest with his left hand. "PP knows that I'm the number one here in Msawawa and he comes second. I'm the real makoya charm. I have great taste in abomabhebeza and I always win them with ease. PP has poor taste when it comes to women. All of his chicks that I know of are shapeless like a two-litre bottle of cooldrink."

"Is that for sure?"

"Siriyasi, man, I'm not lying to you, Advo."

I was tired of talking, but I had to keep going because of the free ride. Luckily I saw Zero's face light up as he stopped the taxi at the red robots by Vista University's Soweto campus. In the other lane was a green Jeep Cherokee and a beautiful young lady with an Afro was driving it. From the open sunroof and windows of the Jeep I could hear the jazz of Moses Molelekwa. Zero immediately wound down his window. He took his 5110 Nokia cellphone from the dashboard and whistled at the lady in the Jeep.

"Hello, Ms Thing," he said to her, smiling.

The lady lowered the volume of her CD player and smiled back at Zero. She waved her hand at him lazily, but Zero had already misinterpreted the lady's innocent smile as a sexual invitation and he smiled again, his mouth spreading from one big ear to the other.

"Oh, my God, you're so fucking hot," he said, running his tongue over his lips, "did you bath in full-cream milk today?"

The lady smiled at the compliment, but she still didn't say anything. Instead she took a drag on the cigarette that she was smoking. Zero pointed at his cellphone as the lady looked at him.

"Can we exchange numbers, mabhebeza? I promise I'll call you tonight."

"Sorry, it's a wrong number," the lady said, trying to lighten her refusal with a smile. "Try next door."

"Why shouldn't I try you, sweetheart? You're the one that I want."

"Because I don't think you have the equipment that I need."

"You're missing out big time, mabhebeza. Don't deprive yourself of the pleasure that I'll give you."

The robots went green and, as the lady sped off, I glimpsed her personalised numberplate that read: *KARABO GP.*

Zero tried to match the speed of the Jeep, but his taxi couldn't keep up. Unfortunately for the lady in the Jeep, the robots were red again at the T-junction leading to Orlando power station. She was looking to her right, at a piece of ground where some shacks had been built, when Zero called to her. It was obvious that he was on the lady's list of no, no, nos, the way she took her time to respond, but Zero wasn't going to give up.

"What's your name, mabhebeza?"

"Syphilis."

"Wow, that's a very nice name. So where do you live, Phyllis?"

I nearly laughed out loud when I realised that Zero hadn't heard the lady correctly.

"I live in Aids View."

"Ace View? Is that a new suburb I don't know?" he asked.

"Yes."

"Where about is that?"

"Between Gonorrhoea Park and Masturbation," she answered, relaxing against the headrest.

"Me and you have a lot in common, mabhebeza," said Zero, grabbing his crotch, "we must get together soon."

"Go jack off," said the lady and took another deep drag on her cigarette.

The robots went green and the lady sped off again.

* * *

By half past nine I was at the Housing Department's offices in Newgate Centre. As I entered, I saw that the corridor was already full of people. The majority had come to register for the low-cost RDP houses that the government was building. There was no way I was going to stand in that queue, so I went straight to the door on which was written *Transfer & Conveyances*. I knocked loudly at the door, just once.

"Come in," said the voice of a woman inside.

I opened the door gently and stepped into the office where two women were busy chatting. The moment I entered the office, the lady sitting behind the table started laughing at a joke her friend had made and I saw that her front tooth was slightly crossed over the one beside it. Her friend, who had slender, long-fingered hands, was holding a white mug of coffee.

"Dumelang," I greeted them in Sotho, as I had heard them speaking the language.

"Dumela, abuti. How can we help you?" said the one with the crooked tooth.

"I was wondering if you could help me by checking if a certain house in Chiawelo, Extension Two, in Soweto, belongs to one Mr Kuzwayo."

The long-fingered lady shook her head and lifted her coffee mug to her lips. She sipped her coffee as she eyed me sharply with the superiority that government office workers show to anybody who's not from parliament.

"What does the title deed say?" she asked, her voice betraying her lack of interest.

"Well, it says it belongs to Mr Sbusiso Kuzwayo."

"Then what's the problem?" asked the one with the crooked tooth.

"I wanted to verify the details because my mother wants to sell it."

The woman with the crooked tooth rubbed the back of her one hand across her eyes.

"Actually, we no longer deal with the transfers of deeds in this office. That stuff must be done privately by the lawyers," her eyes implored me to understand, "so I suggest that you go to your lawyers."

The two ladies immediately returned their attention to their conversation as I walked out of the office. I don't think they even heard me when I thanked them.

As Zero had already returned to Soweto with another load of passengers, I decided to kill time by going to listen to a case at the Johannesburg Magistrate's Court in West Street.

I tiptoed into the back row of Court 5A. The magistrate was reading the indictment in which a lady, Maru Kgama, aged twenty-seven, was accused of having shoplifted some Lil-lets and perfume at one of the Clicks stores in the city centre. Next to the accused was her lawyer who was wearing a black gown and a bib on top of his white shirt. I listened with great curiosity and envy as Mr Charismatic Lawyer convinced the court with ease that it was in the interests of justice that his client did not remain in jail until the date of the trial.

When I left the court about an hour later, my mind was occupied with the depressing thought that I had let my chance to become an advocate slip away.

EIGHT
Friday, December 3

The next day I finished trimming the lawn just before midday. On the grass I put four two-litre plastic bottles, all filled with water. My uncle had suggested that if I did that the township dogs, including Verwoerd, would be too afraid to come and shit on our lawn at night. This was not some township myth, he insisted, it really worked. And I believed him.

As I was busy doing this I saw the postman arrive on his bicycle. He stopped at our gateless driveway and handed me five letters. All of them looked like account letters – I could tell from their cellophane-windowed envelopes even before I opened them. Two of the letters were addressed to me and I immediately opened the one with the UCT stamp on it. Inside the envelope were my official results, which were confirmation of my provisional results. I had failed. The other letter was from the National Student Financial Aid Scheme, and it reminded me that I owed the government R56 000. They had been sponsoring my university studies for four years and now they wanted me to start repaying them. Together with the loan statement was a form that I had to fill in to let them know how much I was going to pay them and the addresses of where I was working and staying.

"Damn it!" I cursed loudly. If the IMF and the World Bank were willing to cancel the debt owed to them by poor African countries, why couldn't our government scratch out the loans owed to it by poor African students like me? Charity must start here, at home.

Uncle Nyawana was standing on the veranda next to his fruit-and-vegetable stall. As usual he was busy writing something in his dream notebook.

"Has your Cape Town girl written to you?" he asked without looking at me.

What my uncle didn't know was that I didn't have a girlfriend, even when I'd been in Cape Town, because I was a slow-approach kind of guy and I was always shy when it came to dating ladies. I didn't have the skill to put romantic words together in an interesting way to charm them like Zero did.

"No, Uncle, it's a letter from NSFAS and another one from Edgars, not from a girlfriend."

"You can't hide it from me, Advo. I heard you cursing someone and I know it's a girl. Long-distance relationships don't work, Advo. That's why you must get a kasi girl. They're easy as ABC to chat up because they like material things. You're lucky because today I'll teach you how to talk these girls out of their panties with ease. After today I'm sure that ladies will be buzzing around you like bees, my laaitie."

"Is that so?" I said uninterestedly, putting my letters in the back pocket of my shorts.

"This is the township, my laaitie, and if you see a lady that you're interested in pass along the street, just stop her by saying, 'Hi, mabhebeza'. I bet she'll be charmed and smile at you. Once you hear her say, 'Hi, my love,' you know it's time to hit hard."

"What do you mean 'hit hard', Uncle?" I asked, curious.

"I mean that you must tell her that you're doing research, as part of your law degree, and that you would like her to show you her arse as part of that research. With your good looks I bet she'll come to your room right away for a nice screw."

"Finding a girl is the least of my worries, Uncle. I have to pay the university so I can get my results and I have to settle my Edgars account before I'm blacklisted."

"Oho! How much do you owe them?"

"I owe Edgars seven clipa, but I owe the university thousands of rands."

"Your mother told me about your results; that you can't have them until you pay big zak. She's very worried about it. But seven hundred for Edgars is not big zak, I think we could make that today if we bet intelligently. Last time we missed very narrowly; we should have played number twenty instead of nineteen," he said, stroking Verwoerd's fur. "What number do you think we should play today?"

"Twenty-nine," I said without thinking, although it occurred to me as I said it that it was actually the percentage that I had scored in my Law of Evidence exam.

"That's why I like you, Advo, you think the same as me. I was thinking of the same number because I dreamt of you having sex with a Hillbrow prostitute last night."

"I'm sure we'll win, Uncle," I said without any conviction.

"I'm confident too. I tell you, if we can play smart for two weeks, we can win thousands and pay what you owe in cash. You see ma-Mshangaan's house? You can't believe that it was an ugly four-roomed house just like ours. Look at it today, Advo! It's a mansion. Can you believe it! She won a lot of money on the fah-fee in June and renovated it."

Before I could respond to my uncle, my cellphone rang. The number that registered on my small screen was a Jo'burg land line. When I answered it I recognised the voice of my university friend Vee. She was a beautiful Zimbabwean lady by the name of Vimbai Mataruse, but I called her Vee. She had also moved to Jo'burg and was now working as a trainee doctor at Milpark Hospital in Auckland Park. Vee and I had gone on three dates when we were students at UCT, but because of my hesitations, nothing concrete had come of it. She called me Bee, short for Bafana.

"Hey, what's up, Bee? Are you still in Cape Town?"

"No, I came back about two weeks ago."

"Guess what?" she said excitedly. "I received my results and I passed all my medicine courses. Not only that, but I came back from Zim the day before yesterday and my work permit has been extended for three months."

"Good for you, girl. Unfortunately, I haven't got mine yet because the university has withheld them," I lied.

"Hectic! What are you going to do now?"

"Well, I was planning to do a diploma in labour or tax law if I got those results, but now I'm going to have to find a job to be able to pay for their release. In the meantime my mother is trying to help me to raise the funds, but congrats again for passing all your courses. When are we going to celebrate your achievements?"

"I'll call you soon. Maybe you can take me out to one of your Soweto restaurants. Most people here at work talk about Wandi's place."

"Good idea!"

"Good! You know I tried to e-mail you about three weeks ago and

I still haven't got a reply from you. Are you still using the same e-mail address?"

"Yes, but I'm in the township and I don't know any internet cafés around here. Do you by any chance know of a cheap one in town? I'm sure my account is full by now as I haven't checked it for a while."

"There's one I use in Yeoville, at the corner of Cavendish and Raleigh. You'll like the rates; it's R4 an hour."

"That sounds very cheap. I'll try to go there soon."

"Okay. Good luck! I've got to go back to work. I'll talk to you soon."

"Okay, bye, Vee."

As I closed the conversation with Vee, a feeling of guilt and re-gret seized me. Regret over all the lies that I had told Vee and my family, and guilt over how I had missed my opportunity to be the first in my family to have a university degree. While thinking about all of this, I smelled the smoke from a zol. When I turned around I saw that my uncle was smoking next to his stall. As he emitted the smoke through his nose and mouth, my uncle sang his own ver-sion of a Bob Marley song.

"No woman no car. No woman no crime," he sang out of tune.

He looked at me and laughed at his own joke with his eyes closed. He seemed to be enjoying himself.

"Get me a music contract today and you'll see the wasted talent in me, Advo. This will be the hottest kwaito song this festive sea-son. You'll produce it and we'll call our group J&B. J for my name, Jabulani, and B for your name, Bafana," he said, laughing again. "We'll conquer the music world!"

He opened his eyes and looked admiringly at his zol.

"This is my Garden of Eden, Advo, I'm eating the fresh fruit of wisdom as I smoke." He emitted some smoke through his nose again and said, as if he had just discovered his own god, "this is my eternal life. Oh, Jah, I love you, baby."

By that time, unseen by my uncle, Priest Mthembu had stopped at our low fence.

"Good afternoon, my sons, how is your day?" said Priest Mthembu, busy opening the top two buttons of his shirt.

"Afternoon, Baba Mfundisi," responded my uncle, dropping his zol on the ground and putting it out with his foot.

"Afternoon to you, my son. The Lord above is great and still guiding us," he said, taking off his hat and looking up into the sky. "Did maTau come to make peace with you yesterday, Jabu? I advised her that she must come over by herself."

"Oh yes, she did, Baba Mfundisi, and we forgave each other," replied my uncle.

"That's good work! Dear God above! Thank you, Amen! That's a good thing done," said Priest Mthembu.

A short silence fell.

"Would you please give me a packet of tomatoes, some onions and a cabbage? You'll get your money over the weekend, my son."

"Yebo, Baba Mfundisi," said Uncle Nyawana.

"Are you busy praying? Don't forget that the millennium is coming," said Priest Mthembu. "There'll be wailing and gnashing of teeth on that day, but only for those who don't praise the Lord. Hallelujah!"

"Amen, Baba Mfundisi," I said.

"And remember Jesus said that those who're last here on earth would be the first in His Kingdom, my sons," said Priest Mthembu as he received his vegetables and walked away.

"Praise the Lord, Baba Mfundisi." My uncle forced the words from his mouth. "But don't forget to make a withdrawal from the bank before the millennium. Advo, my educated nephew here, was telling me that the computers will all crash. If you don't withdraw your money you might lose all your life savings, Baba Mfundisi. You can't trust the white man's banks."

"Thank you, my son, but I've already withdrawn all my money, I did it last week. God bless you! Your kindness will not go unrecognised in heaven."

"'God blast you too, Baba Mfundisi," my uncle shouted after him, without emphasising the letter "t" in the word blast.

I laughed and Uncle Nyawana clicked his tongue.

"Satan! Why isn't he paying me for my vegetables if he has already withdrawn all his zak from the bank?" he said, picking up his zol and trying to light it again. "I'm not here in Chi to serve his God. I'm here to serve my stomach. It's the politics of the belly," he said, lifting his blue T-shirt that was stained with dry sweat.

I saw a thin line of black hair that ran up from his navel to his chest.

"I'm also fighting for my right to get fat like his wife and the chosen few that benefit from Affirmative Action and Black Economic Empowerment," he said, stroking his belly tenderly.

I looked down and smiled.

"I'm forty-three years old, Advo, and I tell you that there's no such thing as God," he whispered. "I believe in Satan because I see his work here in the township every day, but to me God is this." He pointed at his zol. "I swear on my late father, on Sbusiso Kuzwayo's rotting balls there in Avalon Cemetery that there was only one Christian that ever lived on this earth, and that Christian is now dead. And you know who he was, Advo?"

"No, I don't know, Uncle. Who was he?"

"He was that bearded white guy from oorkant called Jesus Christ of Nazareth." My uncle paused and took another puff. "I'm talking about the very same guy from overseas that wrote the Bible in praise of Himself. He was the first, the last and the only Christian that ever lived, and the rest of the people in this kasi that are trying to be like Him are hypocrites."

NINE

Saturday, December 4

In the morning, I was woken up by the rise and fall of two female voices. It was Mama and her friend Zinhle. Sis Zinhle worked as a sister at the Harriet Shezi Children's Clinic at Bara Hospital in Soweto, but it wasn't because of her work that I called her sis. In fact, she had warned me several times that she wasn't old enough to be called Mrs Dube; she was thirty-four years old, six years younger than Mama, and still very attractive.

Carefully, I lifted the lace curtain to peep outside. I saw Mama sitting on a plastic chair under the apricot tree. Her legs rested on the stump of the peach tree that she had asked me to cut down the year before, after some kids had broken my window with stones as they tried to knock down the ripe peaches. Sis Zinhle was busy attacking Mama's head, fitting synthetic hairpieces to make fresh braids.

As I was watching sis Zinhle and Mama, I heard a commotion coming from inside my uncle's room. It sounded like he was busy thrashing his vegetable boxes with one of his crutches.

"Today I got you fools! You have been spoiling my business for a long time!" I heard him complain as if he were talking to a human being.

Quickly, I went to my uncle's room. As I entered, two big rats sprang out of the vegetable box next to his single bed and ran into one corner of the room. My uncle brandished his crutch and tried to hit one of them.

"Do you know how much I spent to buy this stock, you sons and daughters of bitches?" he ranted.

His crutch came slamming down on a big rat that had just sprung out of the dirty pile of clothes under his bed. This time he hit the rat and it screeched with pain.

"Yeah, I got your tail, msunukanyoko!" he continued, uttering his direst curse.

"Who're you talking to, Uncle?" I asked, leaning against the door.

A puzzled expression jumped into his eyes.

"I'm talking to these gatecrashers. They've been eating my business away. I didn't sleep the whole night because they were having an orgy inside my vegetable boxes."

I crouched next to him and together we inspected the damage done by the rats. As soon as I started to check the packs, a fat rat tried to spring out of the box, but my uncle crushed it with his crutch and it fell. He hit it again and it bled. It tried to crawl into the corner of the room, where there was a hole in the cement floor, but before it popped into the hole, my uncle grabbed it by the tail and slung it against the wall with full force. The helpless rat made one last sound and died. Part of the corner of the wall was smeared with blood.

"Wonderful! We've killed the bitch! At least there'll be no more breeding inside this house."

I laughed as my uncle turned the dead rat over with his crutch. With his finicky fingers, each of which was the size of a sausage, he lifted the dead rat by its tail. Its bloody mouth was half open, showing its very sharp front teeth. He frowned at the rat, opened the dining-room door and threw the dead rat near where sis Zinhle was twisting Mama's hair.

"Voetsek, wena, Nyawana," cursed sis Zinhle, "can't you see we're busy here?"

My uncle laughed at them.

"When are you going to grow up?" continued sis Zinhle. "You weren't born with enough brains in your stupid head. Phew, sies!" she said, pretending to be spitting on the ground. "You must work hard to develop your small brain."

* * *

After an hour or so sis Zinhle had finished doing Mama's hair. Mama called me inside my room; she smelled good as always.

"Did you go to the Housing Department?"

"Yes I did, Mama."

"What did you get?"

"I think the house is properly registered, but they suggested that we get a lawyer because the Housing Department no longer does transfers."

Mama began to look nervous at the mention of a lawyer.

"Does your uncle know that I sent you there?" she asked.

"No, you said I mustn't say anything to him, didn't you?"

"Good! Just don't tell him yet . . ."

"But why must I not tell him?" I asked, interrupting her.

"Because I've already got a buyer and I know when to tell your uncle," she said, trying to avoid my question.

"So you don't want to share the money with him?" I asked, but immediately regretted it.

"I'm doing this for you, Bafana," she said angrily. "If I share the money there won't be enough left for you to pay for your results."

She looked at me for a while before walking outside.

When I followed her I saw my uncle was on the veranda putting some vegetables inside small plastic bags. I sat down and watched him. In each packet he put four of the same vegetables. Within a while there were about twenty small plastic bags.

"Let me tell you who my biggest customers are, Advo. You know the shacks at Protea North?" he asked, not looking at me. "They're my biggest clients. You know why?"

"Why?"

"Because most of them don't have refrigerators inside their zo-zos. If they buy in bulk, their vegetables will rot, so they have to buy every day, you see. All these vegetables will be finished by the end of the day, I swear to you."

Not long after that, Mama and sis Zinhle left for Naturena to do some baking. About ten minutes after they had left, three ladies who looked like they were about nineteen came by. Two of them were thin and had dreadlocks, but the third one, who was fatter than the other two, didn't. She had small eyes and a sharply pointed nose; her face had missed the word *beautiful* by half a per cent. One of the girls with dreadlocks had a tiny waist and a flat stomach. The other one had a pierced tongue and small, high breasts. Her ears were also pierced in four places and she wore earrings.

I didn't like the girls instinctively; they were the kind I didn't care to know. Looking at the way they talked and behaved, I could tell that I would have to make a very big adjustment if I wanted to live in the township again.

"Hello, my catalogue girls," my uncle said tenderly. "What can I do for my models today?"

"The usual. We want traditional bio slims. Do you still have some?" asked the one slim girl with dreadlocks. Her legs had some black spots on them that looked like cigarette burns.

"Of course, for sure I've got some. How many do you want today?"

"Two."

"You should take three because you're also three," said my uncle.

"We don't have enough cash, bra Nyawana."

My uncle picked two bags of tomatoes from the box by his foot. I noticed that he avoided the ones that were on the stand. Inside the bags, together with the tomatoes, were two small green envelopes.

As my uncle turned back towards them, I noticed that one of the girls was staring at the blue T-shirt that I had bought for him as a present. He hadn't taken it off his body since I had given it to him more than a week earlier. The T-shirt had *UCT LAW SCHOOL* printed on the front.

"That's nice," the lady pointed at my uncle's T-shirt, "where did you get it, bra Nyawana?"

The lady was so thin that I thought she must be on a perpetual diet. With her equally thin fingers she tried to fix her underwear. It seemed that it wasn't covering enough of her small assets inside her skinny jeans. Instead of answering her question, my uncle turned around to show her the back of his T-shirt, which had *NO COMMENT UNTIL I CONSULT MY LAWYER* printed on it.

The girl smiled.

"Your eyes are sharp for beautiful things, my model. I think you must follow a career in fashion design," he said.

"Thank you," said the girl, blushing at the compliment.

"Let me tell you the truth. If something doesn't fit me well or looks ugly on my body, it means that the designers are not good enough," he continued, smiling at the girls. "Every piece of cloth looks perfect on me, except for the badly designed ones, of course."

"But you still haven't told us where you got the T-shirt from. Or were you a UCT student before?" the pierced one continued sarcastically.

At the mention of UCT I saw the hint of a smile on my uncle's lips. Suddenly his mood had changed.

"Oh, you're fortunate, my catalogue girls, you know that? My well-learned nephew is here. He's going to be the biggest advocate in the whole of Chi," he announced proudly.

My uncle had lived in Chiawelo his whole life and liked bragging that he was among the first people to dub Chiawelo "Chi".

"Wow! Is he your nephew? The brother is yummy, he has good looks! What's his name?" said the pierced one, moving her lips the way Cape Town prostitutes along Main Road did at night.

"His name is Advo," said my uncle as he took R10 from the lady. "I can see that you girls want to screw my nephew, but before you can do that, you'll have to forward your applications to me. This is my sister's precious gift," he laughed and slapped me vigorously on the back.

"Why are you protective of him? Can't he talk for himself?" asked the pierced one.

"Because I don't want any mistakes. You'll have to have a blood test before you apply to be screwed by him. Then I'll let him sleep with all three of you at the same time."

"What are you implying, bra Nyawana? That we have the HIV?" asked the fattish one.

"I mean that young ladies, like you, always want to loosen your panties when you see my handsome nephew, and I don't want my laaitie to die young of Aids. He's got a clean bill of health. You can see that for yourself from his smooth face. It's like he uses a brick of cheese and fresh milk instead of soap and water when he takes a bath."

After the girls had left, my uncle limped inside his room and came back with a bottle of whisky.

"What did I tell you, Advo?" he asked me, making himself comfortable. "Here ekasi, ladies are very easy to screw, especially for educated people like you who have a bright future. Just make them laugh, Advo," he said, guzzling his whisky.

TEN
Monday, December 13

The wind was whistling in the green trees along Commissioner Street when the minibus taxi dropped us next to the Gandhi Square Bus Terminus. In front of us I saw a big-arsed lady's skirt lifted up to her navel by the wind, exposing her full cotton bloomers, but I pretended not to have noticed when Mama looked at me.

It was difficult to penetrate Mama's mind as she hadn't uttered a single word all morning, but her silence was becoming oppressive, sending my mind on a long journey across all the great opportunities that I had wasted by failing my degree.

We waited for the green man to appear on the robots. After a blue-and-grey double-decker Metro bus had come to a halt between Commissioner and Joubert Streets, we crossed and entered an old brown building. Mama's lawyer, Mr Ngwenya, had invited her to his office in the city centre.

As we came out of the lift on the third floor, I saw a piece of paper that had been pinned to the wooden door of Mr Ngwenya's office. It had his name typed on it, as well as the word *Associate*. Out of nowhere jealousy went through me like a sword.

Mr Ngwenya's office was a small, simple space that consisted of two rooms. As we entered the reception area, a lady of about twenty was sitting behind the desk typing on her computer. The first thing I noticed about her was that she had an unusually long neck. Next to her was a television set that was showing the repeat of yesterday's drama series. There were files all over her desk.

"Good morning, my name is Rea Kuzwayo," Mama introduced herself to the lady. "We've an appointment with Mr Ngwenya for eleven o'clock."

The lady glanced at her wristwatch before standing up and opening the door to our right. While she was still standing and talking to someone in the other room, I noticed that she also had unusually long legs. She finished her conversation and ushered us into the office where a guy with acne-scarred cheeks was sitting behind the desk. He was wearing glasses, but his desk didn't have a computer. We sat on the two mismatched chairs opposite him.

"Ms Kuzwayo," started Mr Ngwenya after the formalities, "there are some complications to do with the sale of the house. Mr Sekoto has lodged a complaint with the local housing council through his lawyers."

"Complicated! Just like that!" Mama snapped her fingers and it was obvious from the tone of her voice that the information had infuriated her. "What's that supposed to mean, huh? Bafana told me just the other day that the house was registered under my father's name, didn't you, Bafana?"

"Yes, I did," I nodded.

"But after some careful research that I conducted on my own, I found that the process of the transfer of the title had not been done in the proper way," continued Mr Ngwenya.

"What's that supposed to mean?"

"It means that when we checked the records of your house, we found that Mr Kuzwayo was not the rightful occupant of that house. It turns out that the rightful occupant is also the permit holder of the house, and that is Mr Sekoto. Therefore, if we look at the rights of the council house occupants or lessees, Mr Sekoto would have been the rightful owner of the house according to the Conversion of Certain Rights to Leasehold Act."

The reality of my complicated family history was beginning to emerge, and I could read the doubt starting to creep into Mama's mind as she cleared her throat.

"So what are our chances of winning this case?"

"The chances are fifty-fifty, Ms Kuzwayo. We might argue this case by saying that although Mr Sekoto was technically the rightful occupier of the house since 1971, he never owned it. This is because since 1968 black people had no legal title to the land that they occupied in urban areas like Soweto. Therefore, the house that Mr Sekoto occupied in Chiawelo, which is the centre of contention here, belonged to the council until the 10th of June in 1989. That's the year in which the council itself decided to sell it to Mr Kuzwayo, your father. By the time the Land Tenure Act was repealed in 1986, so that black people could start owning land in urban areas, Mr Sekoto didn't have the legal capacity to do so. That's because he had been committed to Weskoppies Mental Hospital in Pretoria in 1979."

I saw Mama's face flash with delight, but her smile dried up quickly when Mr Ngwenya continued.

"But although your father was the rightful subtenant of Mr Sekoto, for almost two-and-a-half decades, there's a technicality in this matter that makes it tricky. Your father was not the rightful occupant and, as such, the title deed of the house should not have been bestowed upon him."

"So, whose fault is that?"

"Well, your father submitted false documents to the local housing council and that's how he was given ownership."

He looked at Mama again and leaned forward.

"The problem, Ms Kuzwayo," he said, talking slowly as if he were worried about hurting her feelings, "is that Mr Sekoto's lawyers have asked the council to also investigate another matter involving your brothers, Jabulani and Nkosana."

"What did they do now?"

"This concerns the RDP houses that the government has allocated to them."

"What about them?"

"There's this housing scam in the township whereby corrupt local housing officials are paid a certain amount of money in return for allocating low-cost houses. In other words, they sell these houses instead of allocating them to their rightful owners. It seems that Mr Sekoto's lawyers are trying to prove that your family has a history of corruption."

"In other words, you're saying that my brothers' RDP houses in Snake Park and Slovoville are not theirs?" Mama asked with a forced calmness in her voice.

"I'm afraid so. They paid about R1 000 each to two corrupt officials. In return, those corrupt officials scratched out the original owners' names and put your brothers on the list as beneficiaries. They were actually not on the original list," said Mr Ngwenya, consulting a file next to him.

Mama looked away in disbelief.

"Those RDP houses originally belonged to Linda Motaung from Orlando East and Gugulethu Marumo from Meadowlands Zone 7 respectively," Mr Ngwenya continued with great confidence. "But now they're under you brothers' names. It seems Mr Sekoto's lawyers have blown the whistle on the corrupt officials and contacted these people to lodge a claim against your brothers. Apparently, they were very angry when they heard that their houses had been unlawfully taken away by your brothers."

Things were getting stranger and I drew back in shock. I had realised that I didn't know my family that well. I was sure about that now. Trying to understand what had happened was like trying to put a broken mirror back together again.

At that moment, Mama put her elbows on the table next to her handbag as if she were guarding it. It was obvious that the revelations about her brothers had unnerved her; she suddenly looked haggard and sun-blackened. She unzipped her handbag, searched it and came out with some tissue paper that she used to blow her nose. All the time her eyes were fixed on me as if she were imploring me to say something to Mr Ngwenya.

"But that's similar facts evidence," I said bravely, as if I were involved in a cross-examination with Mr Ngwenya in a court of law, "it's inadmissible and irrelevant to this case."

"Wow, that's a good one. I'm very impressed! Did you do law?" he asked with a hint of sarcasm in his tone.

"Yes," I replied.

"Where?"

"The University of Cape Town."

"That's excellent," he said, smiling without humour, "but I'm sure you were taught that similar facts evidence could be admissible if it's legally relevant. If you had an iota of understanding of court procedures you'd know that the relevance in this case is that both your uncles, Nkosana and Jabulani Kuzwayo, as well as your mother here, are co-owners of your Chiawelo home since their father passed away." He paused and angled his face towards Mama. "For argument's sake, let's say co-owners in inverted commas because that's what is contested now. Ms Kuzwayo cannot sell the house without the consent of the other co-owners, who, in this case, are her brothers. In other words, she must go and seek their consent, in the form of their signatures, before she can even think of selling the house. She can't do it on her own."

I was drained to the marrow and felt some sweat trickle down my back. I didn't expect him to expose me like that in front of Mama. My heart was pounding as I tried to reason around the problem. I knew that Mama was expecting me to say something else to Mr Ngwenya.

"Yes, but although my uncles are the co-owners of the house, they gained that status through inheritance, not illegal means," I started, looking at Mr Ngwenya. "So there's no connection between them getting their RDP houses through corrupt means and our family house through inheritance. They can't be held responsible for the conduct of their late father," I said, stating the obvious.

"You're right. All that I am doing is to show where this case might lead, as it might raise many issues from the past. You might end up winning or losing. One of the officials from the Housing Department has already admitted that he was corrupt. His initial argument, that he had passed the ownership of the house on to your uncle simply because the rightful owner didn't come forth to claim it, didn't hold water. In fact, he didn't even call to tell them that their house was ready. That's why he's been suspended."

I nodded and looked at Mama, my eyes imploring her to get things in order, but it seemed she had read the signs. With a pained look on her face, she leaned forward across the table. I switched my eyes from her and looked across the table at Mr Ngwenya.

"So, what do you suggest we do?" Mama asked.

"I was thinking of an out-of-court settlement. You could sell the house after getting your brothers' written consent and then share the profits from the sale with Mr Sekoto."

"What?" Mama asked with annoyance on her face.

"Well, it's entirely up to you, Ms Kuzwayo. I can negotiate with his lawyers if you like, or you can take the risk and proceed."

Mama frowned and I nodded.

"Give me time to think about it, okay?" she finally said.

I felt the bile of guilt in my throat as we left. It was like Mama and I were conspiring against my uncles to do something wrong that seemed right.

* * *

That afternoon I parted with Mama at President Street as she went to pay her account at Woolworths. I elbowed my way down the congested pavement, forcing my way past the street barbers, cobblers, tailors, fake-label clothes sellers and fruit-and-vegetable vendors to a nearby taxi rank. I was on my way to the internet café at the corner of Cavendish and Raleigh Streets in Yeoville, the one that Vee had recommended to me. I wanted to send my first job application letter, as well as my CV, to the address that Mama had given me. Besides wanting Mama to think I was serious about finding a job, I also wanted to check my e-mail account.

The internet café was very small. There were about eight black guys inside, speaking a language I didn't understand; they were all glued to their computer screens as if they were writing manifestos on the African Renaissance.

"Nwanne! Do you want to use a computer that has a diskette or one without?" asked a tall guy with a heavy Nigerian accent.

"I would like to use a computer with a diskette, please. There's an attachment that I want to send," I answered, carefully avoiding the first word of his question which I didn't understand.

"You'll have to wait five minutes. That guy over there will finish just now," he said, checking the time on his cellphone.

He showed me a stool to sit on while I waited for the other guy to finish using the computer. In the meantime I took out the paper with the job advert in it and read it again. Mama had insisted that I apply to be a legal advisor even though I didn't have the necessary experience. I had nothing to lose in applying and, besides, my life had become directionless in the township and I knew I didn't have the capabilities to survive the monotony. I needed a job.

"I know most of my customers, but I haven't seen you in this shop before. My name is Yomi, and welcome to the shop, umunne," said the tall guy, extending his hand.

"Heita. I'm Bafana, and it's my first time here."

"How did you get to know about this place?" he asked.

"I have a friend called Vimbai, she's the one that recommended it to me."

"I know Vee. She comes here every weekend. Are you also from Zim?"

"No, I'm a South African, from Soweto."

"Ah, I know Soweto," he said with interest in his voice. "I once had a shop at the Dobsonville Mall, but I closed it. The police were harassing me left, right and centre, nwanne. They always wanted me to pay a bribe, saying that I'm a kwere-kwere. Xenophobia is real in this country, I've seen it. Even when I showed them my resident's permit they wouldn't leave me alone. When I refused, they raided my shop every day saying that I sell drugs."

He paused to see if I was still listening.

"Umunne, it's hard to do business in this country if you're a foreigner," he continued, "especially from Nigeria. But I'm looking at expanding my internet services in Soweto again and that is why I'm searching for someone from there to run it for me. I wish we can talk sometime about the matter, nwanne. Which part of Soweto do you come from?"

"I'm from Chi."

"I know Chi. Give me your contacts before you leave and perhaps we can talk the business, umunne."

The guy sitting in the corner finished using the computer and immediately after removing his diskette, Yomi helped me to log in. I sat there for about an hour. I had thirty unread messages in my inbox.

* * *

At about four in the afternoon I was at the Noord Street Taxi Rank waiting for Zero's taxi together with the overworked and underpaid passengers. I didn't want to pay for the taxi fare, as usual, and Zero gave me a free ride without complaint on account of my new-found fame as an advocate.

It started to rain as we passed the Chicken Licken outlet in Booysens. Next to the police station the robots weren't working and a female traffic official stood in the middle of the road directing the traffic. I was sitting in the front seat, staring absent-mindedly out of the taxi's closed window as the cars blurred past us in the opposite direction. Between Zero and myself was a fat lady with a beautiful face. I concluded that she had been a hot number during her youth.

"These tow trucks are at it again, Advo. Haaa! Amazing! Even here the robots are not working? I thought it only happened in the townships," Zero complained.

"What do tow trucks have to do with it?" I asked wearily.

"You want to tell me that you don't know why the Soweto Highway is nicknamed The Killer Road, Advo? It's because the tow trucks employ the street kids to fiddle with the robots. After the accident they tow the cars away to their scrapyards and charge you big zak to get them back. If you fail to pay, they sell your car," he said, accelerating as the traffic officer raised her left hand to allow us to move forward.

"Is that so? I wasn't aware that they did that."

"Siriyasi, Advo! That's why I don't give money to these street kids at the robots."

The woman between us cleared her throat, a sound of disapproval. Zero glanced at his wing mirror again and then back at the road.

"That sounds horrible," I said.

"Those sons of monkeys are dirty suckers, that's what they are. Tow truckers are like hungry vultures, Advo. They wait for an accident to happen like a fish eagle waits for a fish in the river: with clawed feet, a very sharp beak and hungry eyes. If an accident happened right now, oh, I bet they'd be here within the wink of an eye. When it's raining like this it's even worse, Advo, because it's good for their business. They spill oil on the road, so that even if your car has ABS you can't avoid an accident."

I stared at the scar on Zero's head as if it had been caused by one of the accidents that he was talking about. It was an old wound just above his left ear.

"Those vultures work hand in glove with corrupt cops and street kids," Zero continued. "They have police walkie-talkies and the moment you call the police to the scene of an accident, they intercept the call."

"I didn't know that."

"Siriyasi, Advo! You know that boy who lives next door to where I used to rent a back room in Chi? He's now in jail there at Sun City."

"Is that so? Is the kid in prison now?" I asked, thrusting the tip of my finger into my ear and shaking it.

"I thought that you knew about that. I heard his mother mentioning that she was coming to talk to you about representing her son for free."

"Me, representing him for free?"

We were now in Soweto, on the Old Potch Road in Dlamini Section, and some of the passengers inside the taxi shouted "short left". Zero stopped the taxi for the passengers to step out.

"Ja, that boy is underage. He's only thirteen. They say it's the first time that he's committed an offence, but he has admitted that he was paid R100 per accident by an Indaba tow-truck driver."

"That's bad. I haven't heard anything from his mother, though."

"That's because he was sentenced already."

"Sentenced? Where? I mean the boy is very young, is he in juvenile prison or what?"

"He does community service at a government mortuary somewhere in town," said Zero, laughing.

If the lady between us was impressed, she didn't show it at all as she just shrugged.

"He's washing the corpses," Zero continued, his voice devoid of forgiveness.

"But he's too young to do that . . ." I said.

"I think it's the right sentence. That boy has corpses under his name on this soil."

Having to listen to Zero's conversation was an experience in itself, but I was happy that we were now in Chi, where it hadn't rained at all. Darkness was beginning to swallow the day when I got out of his taxi at the Mangalani BP Garage.

ELEVEN
Friday, December 17

That Friday it was Mama's turn to hold the monthly stokvel. In the morning, before everyone arrived, Mama called us into my uncle's room to talk about selling the house. My sister, Nina, was there as well, looking pretty in her embroidered bootleg jeans and multi-coloured V-neck T-shirt and with her shoulder-length dreadlocks.

Nina had a two-year-old son with her boyfriend, Bheki. She had had a very big fight with Mama when she had fallen pregnant aged eighteen. According to Nina, she was still in a cooling-off period away from home, but she had agreed to come over to talk about selling the house.

Mama and Nina were sitting in Uncle Nyawana's room on the white plastic chairs that they had removed from the kitchen; Uncle Nyawana and Yuri sat on his single bed which creaked each time they twisted and turned. I avoided sitting on the bed because its sponge was old and uncomfortable. My sister had long ago nick-named uncle Nyawana's bed the Titanic, after the famous movie, and even Yuri, light as he was, appeared to be sinking ever further into it as he sat there. My uncle had not yet made his bed and there were also clothes jumbled all over it. The smell of stale sweat lay thick in the air.

"I called all of you this morning because we have a problem, and it concerns Bafana," Mama started, looking at me. "As you already know, he doesn't have his results yet because he owes the university money."

"It's a pity that I'm not working, my Advo. Otherwise, you know that I would pay," said my uncle. "But maybe we can club together to help you. My grant money only comes on the last day of the month, but I'm sure I can give you five hundred bucks."

"I can try to come with a R1 000 this month because I'm getting my birthday bonus cheque," offered Nina.

Mama looked at both of them as she spoke again. My uncle listened while at the same time cracking his knuckles. He then reached for a cigarette next to his thin pillow and lit it, and it immediately overpowered all the bad smells in the room.

"Listen, he has to get these results soon, so that he can start practising as an advocate. I appreciate the idea of putting some money together, but it won't be enough. We might starve before we came up with the twenty-two thousand that he owes," said Mama, her gaze never leaving my face.

"What is on your mind, Mama?" asked Nina.

"I was thinking of a major sacrifice from you both. I have been thinking, Jabu, since both you brothers have RDP houses, you won't have much of a problem with helping your nephew in that regard. I want us to sell this house so that we can raise some money."

"What? Sell the house?" my uncle fumed. "I know you, Rea! You're intimidated by the old man Sekoto."

"It's not like that," Mama said, trying to stay calm. "I want Bafana to get his results . . ."

"Then speak to Guava and ask if we can sell his RDP house."

"We can't sell an RDP house, it's illegal," said Mama as two shiny cockroaches passed between her feet and disappeared somewhere under the bed.

"Let's play fah-fee then, I know we can win if we concentrate. Imagine if we bet a thousand bucks. We could win a lot of money."

Nina and I laughed, but Mama was not impressed. Yuri tried to swat away the fly that had just settled on his lower lip, but he ended up slapping his own mouth.

Meanwhile, outside the house, PP and Dilika's arrival was marked by TKZee's "Izinja zami", which they were playing at an ear-shattering level.

"Come on, Jabu, be serious," Mama pleaded.

"I have a lot of business interest in this house, Rea. We can't sell it," said my uncle, his concentration disturbed by the loud kwaito outside.

"You're being selfish, Jabu," she said, giving him a look that would have melted ice cubes.

"Selfish? That is brother abuse!" my uncle said, storming out of the room as Mama fired words of blackmail after him.

"What kind of a selfish brother are you? A brother who can't even sacrifice for his nephew! You're a hypocrite, Jabu! Like it or not, this house is going to be sold! I have already spoken to brother Guava about it," she lied.

"You and Guava are betraying me! That is betrayal of brotherhood!"

"You're not a true brother, Jabu! You're a selfish brother!"

"That is brother exploitation!" he fired back as he limped out of the house.

"You . . ." She stopped, as if she didn't have the heart to finish her sentence.

I went outside while Nina, Mama and Yuri remained in the house

84

to prepare for the stokvel party. I sat on the plastic chair under the apricot tree next to my uncle, Dilika and PP. My uncle was holding a piece of paper torn from the page of an old issue of the *Sowetan* newspaper and removing the seeds from his zol as he prepared to roll it. Behind his chair was a fresh mound of Verwoerd's shit that was still steaming.

MaMfundisi and four other women, who were also members of Mama's stokvel group, arrived and went inside the house after greeting us. Sis Zinhle also arrived in her car with four more women, and they all sat with us under the apricot tree without joining the other women in the kitchen. The women all looked beautiful, but sis Zinhle was outstanding in her brown wrapover top, straight-leg jeans and brown peep-toe shoes. All the women were members of Mama's stokvel group of twelve, and each one of them had contributed about R250. The only person missing was sis Dudu, Uncle Nyawana's ex-wife, but she had sent her money with sis Zinhle.

The food that they cooked was to be sold to non-members like Dilika, PP, my uncle and all the other men. It was R20 a plate. I was asked by Mama to help her sell the drinks that were locked inside my room in two large steel baths. I was to sell the ciders and beers at R4 a dumpy. Mama was convinced that she could make some profit to help me pay some of the money that I owed to the university if the deal of the house didn't go through.

PP offered to buy all five women ciders and he also bought beers for himself, Dilika and my uncle. After giving me a R100 note, I went inside my room to collect his order. When I came out of the house, Mama was already sitting there on the grass mat together with sis Zinhle and the other women. Yuri was sitting next to her and, as I put the drinks in front of PP, he started coughing painfully in a high-pitched tone that sounded like a cat.

"Chomza, are those pills that I gave you for him finished?" asked sis Zinhle. "It seems his illness is worse this week."

Before Mama could answer, Uncle Nyawana, who had finished rolling his joint, shook his head vigorously to express his disapproval.

"I don't even want to see those pills because they're the ones that cause Aids. They killed my sister, his mother, Thandi, two years ago after she had started to use them. If I had known that they had toxic side effects, I would have discouraged her from using them right from the word go. Those things don't stop Aids, and the politicians are just lying to us about them."

There was a great chorus of discontent from all of the women, but it was sis Zinhle who responded.

"No one has ever said that ARVs cured Aids," she said. "They only produce short-term benefits for seriously sick people like him." She pointed at Yuri. "If it wasn't for the ARVs, I think he would be no more by now."

"Zinhle, I don't believe that you, an educated person, also accept that lie. Look at Yuri now! He sometimes suffers from epilepsy because of those pills that you're feeding him. If I happen to get that disease myself I want you to do me a favour, please . . ." My uncle paused and lit his zol. "Do not feed me those pills because they're useless. They don't cure Aids! And that's my final wish."

"Suit yourself! But I don't think you'll ever catch the disease because, since Dudu left you, you haven't had a girlfriend," Mama chipped in, as if she were retaliating for their earlier fight. All the women laughed.

86

Sis Dudu was Uncle Nyawana's ex-wife who now lived in Vietnam in Naledi Extension. They had been married for about four years and had a nine-year-old daughter called Palesa. Sis Dudu had left my uncle some six years earlier and now worked at Clicks in Highgate. Although she had not remarried and was still living with her family, I'd heard from Mama that sis Dudu had had another child by another man. Her son was now five years old.

Uncle Nyawana ignored the laughter and passed his zol to PP, emitting smoke through his mouth and nose as he did so.

"Read my lips! Like I was telling you the other day, bra PP, these modern medicines don't work. My mother used to have all kinds of different medicines when I was young. No one was ever sick in my home," said Dilika, after taking a sip from his beer. "I remember uswazi, umdubu, amasethole, umkhele, umusuzwane, ihlungunhlungu . . . Oh, man! I could count until tomorrow. Those were helpful medicines. Not this modern stuff without a name."

"Oh, bra Dilika, nkalakatha! You remind me of my traditional doctor, uBaba Ngema. You know that sangoma of mine has just given me a powerful medicine. It's so potent that I can't get sick, even if I sleep with prostitutes without a condom," said PP.

"You're the man, bra PP. I must also visit Madlokovu to get that stuff," said my uncle.

I went to my room quickly and came out again with the beer orders for the four men that had just arrived with their women. Because of the lack of space under the tree, the new arrivals were sitting in the shade under the wall of the house and having their own separate conversation. When I got back to the tree, sis Zinhle was talking.

"Yes, tell them, chomza," said Mama. "These men think that they're clever, mentioning all their traditional medicines."

"Mentioning traditional medicines doesn't help if they cannot cure the disease. It's like me mentioning the names of all the anti-retroviral drugs and then claiming that they can cure Aids," sis Zinhle said.

"Read my lips, Zinhle! Why not mention them if you believe in them, huh?" Dilika asked.

"Because then I'd be lying to you because I know that they have side effects. I could also mention Stavudine, Zerit, Zidovudine, Nevirapine . . . I can also count until tomorrow like you, but if I didn't tell you that they have side effects such as diarrhoea, heartburn, vomiting, extreme tiredness, depression and so on, I'd be lying to you."

There was silence while Nina and three women came out of the house carrying the food that PP had ordered for Dilika and my uncle. Yuri smiled and wriggled his small toes. He seemed calm on Mama's lap. She was cuddling him as if he were a corpse that she didn't want to bury.

"Read my lips! Let me tell you people," said Dilika, with food in his mouth. "The right medicine for Aids is available, but it's not for sale here in Africa. Has anybody heard of anyone dying of Aids in Europe or America? The death rate is very low that side of God's world because there is a cure, but here in Satan's Africa the medicine is not for sale because the scientists see a long-term profit in letting Africans die. These bastards developed the virus as a biological weapon against us Africans, and that's why we won't make it. We will continue to die like flies!" he continued, brushing off two flies that looked like they were screwing on the edge of his plate.

I watched Dilika as he dismissed Verwoerd with the back of his hand.

"Tell them, Dilika, nkalakatha!" shouted my uncle.

"That's a pure lie," said Mama without thinking. "There are a number of celebrities that I have read of in magazines that are dying of the virus overseas."

"Read my lips, Rea!" said Dilika, moulding his pap into a small white ball between his fingers. "Aids is no longer a death sentence in most First World countries," he paused and dipped the small ball of pap into the gravy, "because the world is divided into continents where the disease is survivable and where it's not," he concluded, swallowing loudly.

"Stop arguing, because the only thing that cures your Aids is this," said Uncle Nyawana, rolling another zol with another piece of old newspaper. "It's not the viral pill that you're busy talking about that stops Aids, but this zol here," he repeated, licking the edges of the paper.

Evening was already spreading itself over the excruciatingly hot afternoon when Mama, sis Zinhle and Yuri left for Naturena in sis Zinhle's car. Nina had long gone, but my uncle and his friends were still sitting in their chairs, weaving in and out of sleep. They were quite drunk.

Thirty minutes later there was a sudden gust of wind that made the clothes on the Jobe's washing line across the street flap loudly. PP and Dilika woke up and staggered towards the car and drove off. My uncle limped into his room and when I went into his room later, I saw his one foot dangling over the edge of his old single bed. He was snoring loudly.

TWELVE
Saturday, December 18

Mama came to Chi early the next morning so that I could help her count the profits of the previous day's stokvel. She had hidden the money we had made under my bed and, by the time she arrived, I had managed to steal about R150 from the bag.

"This matter is stressing me," said Mama, sighing. "Yesterday afternoon, after the stokvel, Mr Ngwenya called me to say that the Department of Housing has acknowledged that it was at fault for transferring the house in our name. To remedy the situation they've promised Mr Sekoto another house somewhere in Protea Glen and he has agreed to take it as a compromise."

"At least he has another roof over his head."

"Yeah, but Mr Ngwenya also told me that both of your uncles have lost their RDP houses and they don't even know about it."

My guilt was increasing with each day that passed, and the urge to confess to Mama that I had failed was becoming irresistible.

"But Mama, I feel guilty that . . ." I said, but I couldn't even finish my sentence. Mama tenderly held up her index finger to my mouth, commanding my silence.

"Shhhh! I know, my baby," she comforted me, her sweaty face flushed with love. "Don't worry, everything will be fine soon. I'll find a way to convince him."

After we had finished counting the coins, Uncle Nyawana came back from betting on the horses at Mangalani TAB. Mama had made just over R3 400. She was very happy about it.

As I went out to join my uncle, there were the same girls that had come to buy bio slim a couple of weeks earlier. My uncle smelt of armpit and his back was slick with sweat.

"These girls come here for the same thing every week. What's bio slim anyway?" I asked after the girls had left.

"That's dagga, Advo. Living in Cape Town has made you forget most of our slang."

"Those girls smoke dagga?"

"Don't you know that it's a fashion nowadays? It's for girls that are obsessed with losing weight. I put it inside the tomato bags, for my real customers, so that when the police raid my stall they don't realise that I'm the snyman who sells dagga here." He adjusted the filthy cloth that he had put on the stump of his amputated leg. "Those girls come all the way from Vietnam, from the same street as my ex-wife, Dudu, because I've got good Swazi poison. But, hey, don't tell your mother that I sell dagga here. I'm just teaching you the business so that when I'm away you can continue selling for me. That's the reason I don't want us to sell this house, Advo, because business is booming. Your mother doesn't understand!"

Mama was busy cleaning up the mess in the yard from the stokvel when sis Zinhle arrived in her VW Golf. She parked it on the pavement.

"But those girls that were here just now are really beautiful, aren't they, Advo?" asked Uncle Nyawana.

"They are, Uncle."

"Which one of them did you like?"

"No one."

"Don't worry, I'll organise one for you tonight. Here in Soweto I'm the only one who is networked with beautiful girls, my Advo . . ." He paused and then corrected himself. "Well, my friend PP and Zero are connected as well, but I know why PP has children all over Mzansi. It's because of the child welfare system. Since it started, young girls want to have kids with any man. Then they claim the child grant from the Welfare Department as well as financial support from the father every month. Double payment, you see, Advo?"

I was aware that matchmaking was one of my uncle's favourite pastimes. Often, when he saw a couple of young people walk by in the street, he would tell them whether they suited one another or not. He also had a habit of making comments about their weight to the ladies that passed his stall. If he saw a slender lady passing by, he would always suggest that she go and have an HIV test. If a lady he knew looked like she had gained weight, he always assumed that she was pregnant and would ask who the lucky guy was. Luckily, most people overlooked his rudeness and forgave him because he only had one leg.

"Eee-er," I hesitated. "I don't think I really want any of those girls, uncle."

"Nonsense! Why not? Those ladies are all fine. They don't have the kids yet . . . Oh, no!" He paused to correct himself again. "That fattish one with the round face like a soccer ball has got two kids, but the rest of them are all fine, first class."

"They're not my type," I said, without looking up.

"That's nonsense, Advo! Or have you changed into a moffie? I know that those universities in Cape Town teach people to be gay. All gay people come from the Mother City. Are you one of them, Advo?"

"No, Uncle, I just don't like those girls."

"Hey, Advo, having a girl will help you not to be naughty at night. You won't need to self-cater any more once you have a girlfriend."

Without a word, I looked at the bottle of whisky next to my uncle's leg. I knew that the J&B had ruined my uncle's mind for another day.

"Haa, I know you like the girl in the camo pants," he said, dropping two ice cubes into his whisky glass. "She's gorgeous, isn't she, Advo? I saw love at first sight in your eyes."

"No, well, perhaps it was admiration at first sight, Uncle."

"You can't fool me, Advo. Now let me tell you something wise. You know that there is danger in suppressing your feelings for a lady, don't you?" He took a sip of his whisky. "It's like holding a fart in your stomach when you know that you're pressed." He put the glass down. "You must never do that. If you don't release your fart, you allow it to travel up your spine and into your brain," he said. "And you know what, Advo? That's where shitty ideas come from. That's why most boys here in Chi are either gay or rape women and children. It's all because they're afraid to say the three words." He lifted three fingers from his left hand to emphasise what he was saying. "Not 'HIV', but 'I love you'."

PP and Dilika arrived about thirty minutes later while Mama and sis Zinhle were still busy cleaning the yard. The big black dustbin and four refuse bags were full of beer bottles, bones, paper plates and other rubbish. Mama shook her head in disbelief as she picked up the cigarette butts from where my uncle and his friends had been sitting the previous day.

"You people smoke like coal stoves," she complained. "Look what

I have here!" She showed us a handful of cigarette butts. "Your mothers must have taken away their breasts sooner than you wanted."

"Read my lips, Rea! I taught biology at school and I used to tell my students exactly that; that a cigarette is a substitute for a breast. I feel warmth and comfort when I smoke; it's the same as warm milk from a breast. Do you want a cigarette? Here, take it," Dilika offered playfully.

"Excuse me, but I prefer spending my money on food and clothes rather than burning it. If I were you, Jabu, I would stop smoking. You know that you have asthma," Mama warned my uncle.

"Tell him, chomza," said sis Zinhle, throwing a beer bottle in the bin. "Maybe we should alert the government to the fact that his monthly disability grant isn't going on his medication, but to the breweries and cigarette companies."

"You two talk as if it's your money that I'm receiving every month. I'm a loyal citizen and I voted for the ANC in the national *erection* this year in order to get these benefits."

We all laughed, but my uncle ignored us. He was trying to catch the attention of one of the boys that was busy playing soccer in the street. Fortunately for him the tennis ball rolled towards our yard and one of the boys from the group came to fetch it. As the boy picked up the ball, my uncle called him.

"Hey, ntwana, zwakala hier! Go to that house and tell them to give you more ice for my whisky," he said, pointing at the Jobe's house.

Within minutes the boy was back with a plastic container full of ice cubes. He put it down and immediately ran back into the street to join his friends.

At that moment sis Zinhle bent over to pick up a bottle and a cigarette butt next to my window and deposit it in the refuse bag she was holding. As she picked up the bottle, her red cotton bloomers flashed from the waist of her bootleg jeans. I was looking at her trim waist. She was as slim as a young girl.

"Hey, gents, look!" Uncle Nyawana's eyes stopped on me. "Advo has been looking at Zinhle's arse, without blinking, for about three minutes now. I've been watching him!"

I quickly withdrew my eyes and cast them down in embarrassment, but my uncle continued making fun of me.

"My Advo, it seems you and bra PP have something in common," he said in an accusatory tone of voice.

I scratched my head lightly and then threw up my hands in defeat.

"That's the problem with being overeducated: education makes one forget tradition!" Dilika warned me. "Have you forgotten that young boys should never look at the private parts of older women because they'll go blind?"

I paused for a moment to marshal my courage.

"No, I wasn't looking at her," I said.

"Don't worry, Advo. To hell with the tradition!" said PP protectively. "If my father had stuck with those boring old cultural rules, I wouldn't be here today. He was far younger than my ouledi when they got married."

There was laughter and sis Zinhle looked in our direction. That really embarrassed me as I didn't want her to hear our nasty little conversation.

"Don't worry, my Advo. I was only joking with you," said Uncle

Nyawana with a smile pasted on his red lips. "There's nothing wrong with looking at Zinhle's tight arse."

"You're right, my bra," said PP, puffing out smoke from his zol. "Every man here ekasi is trying to get a nice fat slice of arse." He laughed out loud. "Just look at her, gents!" He pointed at sis Zinhle's backside.

The laughter suddenly alerted sis Zinhle to the fact that we were talking about her, and for the first time I felt vulnerable around my uncle and his friends.

"I heard that! What are you staring at, you Dilika?" asked sis Zinhle. "You old farts must stop teaching that innocent boy your ugly horny ways," she said, but not in a serious tone of voice.

"Read my lips! What I'm staring at is none of your bloody business," responded Dilika.

Sis Zinhle looked at Dilika again and tried to pull her jeans up to cover the naked part of her waist. Dilika smiled.

"Where is your respect? Read my lips, you're purposefully trying to fish us by not covering your bloomers."

"And you call yourselves men? I think Bafana is more mature than the three of you combined," retorted sis Zinhle.

"Just shut up, will you? You outdated woman! You're out of fashion like a young lady that still takes snuff. Women of your age no longer wear those full panties like you do! Read my lips! For your information, it is G-string time, baby," said Dilika.

Sis Zinhle and Dilika looked at each other with hatred.

"Fuck you! I had forgotten that you're a useless alcoholic paedophile," said sis Zinhle, sounding malicious, "and that's why the Department of Education has suspended you from your teaching post;

because you like staring at little schoolgirls. How many have you impregnated this year alone?"

We all burst out laughing, but Dilika was not impressed.

"I would like to share your boring joke when you're finished laughing," he said to us. "As for you, Zinhle, read my lips, feel free to go on insulting me, but I can't be held responsible for my reflexes," he said, shame descending on him.

"Nkalakatha, you must just admit that she got you with an uppercut of an insult this time," said PP, ignoring Dilika's anger.

Dilika was not impressed and in a fit of extreme bad temper, he tried to down the entire contents of his glass. As he did so the glass slipped from his hand, fell on the rockery and broke.

"Read my lips! You'll see! All you Msawawa people that are jealous of me and contributed to my downfall through your witchcraft, you'll be humiliated," he insisted. And then, drunkenly, he whispered at my uncle, who lent him his drunken ear. "But no matter what Zinhle says, I used to screw her during my day, my bra," he declared proudly. "I did that girl the greatest favour and she knows it too. I taught her how to fuck while she was in standard seven at Progress High," he continued as he studied sis Zinhle with his lazy drunken eyes. "Read my lips! She was still a virgin, Advo, very tight, and she knew nothing about screwing. And this is the thank you I get from her."

Sis Zinhle went into the house to help Mama wash the dishes. Dilika lifted my uncle's glass and poured some whisky into it before dropping in some ice cubes.

"Read my lips, that was before she got married to that stupid doctor, Mzwakhe," he whispered drunkenly into my ear. "Read my lips!

I think she married him for money because I know Zinhle, Advo. She's always been good at mixing money and romance. Her husband is a chizboy, you see, and his family is loaded with zak. That is why she married him. Whoever says money can't buy love is lying to you, Advo. They must ask Zinhle," he said.

Half an hour later Mama came out of the house with sis Zinhle, and together they left in her car. A short while afterwards PP and Dilika dragged their drunken bodies into PP's BMW.

THIRTEEN
Saturday, December 25

It was ten o'clock on Christmas Day and a popular kwaito song by Mandoza was busy playing loudly from inside PP's BMW. Mama had invited her friends, including sis Zinhle, over to our house for a braai. Uncle Thulani was working, doing the Christmas shift at Sun City. Uncle Nyawana had also called his friends, PP, Dilika and Zero, although the latter was still at work. Vee had called me to say that she would come by after twelve. The only people missing were my sister, Nina, and Uncle Guava, Mama's elder brother.

My sister was staying with her boyfriend, Bheki, and they had organised to spend the day away from us with their friends. Uncle Guava, on the other hand, was serving a jail term in Sun City for arson and for badly assaulting one of our neighbours. Their once beautiful white house was now blackened and roofless. So far he had served only two years of his five-year sentence, but in those two years the owners of the house hadn't returned to it once. They were too afraid of what we might do to them.

Our neighbour's sin had been to spread the rumour in Chi that Aunt Thandi, Yuri's mother, had died of Aids – which was true – but Uncle Guava, who had been a protective brother to my aunt ever since she was young, had accused the old couple of witchcraft. He had doused their house with petrol during the night and set it alight. Luckily no one died, but he was arrested, and that's why he was still in Sun City.

Everyone, including Yuri, my sickly cousin, looked happy that it was Christmas Day. Our street was already buzzing with drunken adults and happy children. I didn't normally pray, but I said a few lines of the Lord's Prayer as I prepared the fire and asked God to make Yuri healthy like the other kids I could see in the street.

While the coal fire was burning I went inside where Mama was busy marinating the meat. I dragged her into my room and showed her the large brown envelope with a cellophane window that had arrived earlier in the week.

"It's from the old man's lawyers. They're still opposing the sale of the house on the grounds that we are not the rightful owners," I whispered to Mama.

"You're kidding me!" Mama said, shaking her head in defeat. "You know I had people who were interested in buying yesterday. What do we do now?"

"Let's wait and see, Mama. The year is almost over. We'll see next year."

"No, come on, Bafana, you can do better than that," pleaded Mama, "you went to the university, you can solve problems like this one. Use those brains! Come on, think!"

"But Mama, there's nothing we can do now. The courts are in recess," I insisted. "The only thing we can do in the meantime is to get Uncle Guava to sign the consent form for the sale of the house."

"That's better. We'll go and see your uncle Guava. Maybe if he signs the papers, Jabu will reconsider."

The fire was ready when I came out with the marinated meat and wors. Uncle Nyawana and his friends, as well as sis Zinhle, were sitting not very far from the fire on the white plastic chairs under the apricot tree. Although she didn't drink much, sis Zinhle had brought a bottle of Amarula Cream, and it was obvious that she was enjoying it. PP was wearing his dark sunglasses and a sporty brown hat. It was easy to tell that drunkenness was setting in by the way he talked.

"I'm Pelepele, the real chilli. Ngishisa bhe! I'm very hot!" he said, punching his chest proudly. "There's just something about me that beautiful women can't resist," he boasted.

"Read my lips, nkalakatha! Women love you because you drive a nice BMW. And I'm sure you know what BMW means," shouted Dilika, flicking his cigarette ash on the ground. "BMW is an abbreviation for Bring More Women; it's the most powerful love potion known here ekasi."

They both broke out laughing and PP even slapped his thigh with contentment. Verwoerd was sitting under my empty chair, with his long tongue hanging out, looking at PP and Dilika without blinking, an almost human expression of confusion on his face. PP and Dilika flipped their thumbs slowly and clapped their hands together while sis Zinhle daintily sipped her Amarula, her lips hardly making contact with the glass.

"You're right, my friend. The judges here in Mzansi know me very well. Yes, here in South Africa, judges respect me a lot," PP said, guzzling his J&B whisky that he had mixed with beer. "And you know why the judges know me, huh?" he asked. "It's because I've sent women to maternity wards all over Mzansi with my joystick. Yes, here in South Africa alone, I've appeared in thirteen maintenance courts. Old women, young women, middle-aged women, flavoured and plain women, sweet, sour, bitter and delicious women; they all can't wait to fit me between their pretty thighs." He raised his fingers in the air as if he were counting. "I've experience in how women reach orgasm in each of our eleven official languages. If I want to listen to my woman reach orgasm in Sesotho during sex, I simply go to my woman in TY, down the Maluti Mountains in Lesotho. In Botswana, Mozambique and Swaziland, I also have maintenance cases pending. I know that they have the death penalty in Botswana, but they can't catch me because I'm too clever. They once tried to catch me in Swaziland, but they soon realised that it was a waste of precious time because I'm a great friend of King Mswati. Even the police know that PP is as slippery as soap inside a bath full of water. Ngiyinsimbi ayigobeki! I'm the steel rod that doesn't bend!"

I was standing next to the braai, turning the roasting meat with a long barbecue fork. Uncle Nyawana was sitting on top of an upside-down beer crate listening quietly to his friend PP. Mama and sis Zinhle were sitting on a grass mat that was spread on the trimmed lawn. Mama was wearing a dress with a Basotho Seshweshwe print; sis Zinhle was in a blue skirt and T-shirt. Yuri sat on the pillowed sanctuary of sis Zinhle's appetising thighs. He was chewing the piece of meat that I had just given him as a bribe to stay away from the fire. I watched him toss a bone to Verwoerd, who caught it in midair before chewing and swallowing it.

"Yeah, I tell you, I've turned thousands of women's stomach muscles to jelly with this," continued PP, pointing between his thighs as if the greatest tool of creation ever known was concealed there.

As sis Zinhle stood up and walked towards the kitchen door, PP turned to my uncle and said, "You see Zinhle's slender figure, nkalakatha?" My eyes followed PP's hands as he described sis Zinhle's figure. "I bet you that I can destroy it in two hours with my weapon of mass destruction. The only reason I've spared her all this time is that she's light-skinned. I prefer my women hot and black, just like my coffee."

He pulled out a pack of the red-striped Stuyvesants and offered my uncle and Dilika a cigarette each.

"You, PP, like to belittle women and I hope that one of these days they put you in jail for a very long time," protested sis Zinhle as soon as she returned from the kitchen with the chicken pieces for the braai. "When you come out I bet you'll have learnt how to respect women."

"Ha!" PP gave a scornful laugh. "Me, prison again? That's impossible, and you know why? This is PP, the real Pelepele. Ngishisa bhe! I'm very hot! Here in Mzansi money talks. If you have money you can always win your case here in South Africa through what lawyers like Advo here call creative diplomacy. And you know what that is?"

"No idea, I've not been to jail like you, remember?" said sis Zinhle.

"You don't even know what creative diplomacy is?"

Sis Zinhle shook her head while PP sucked on his cigarette.

"Come on, Advo, tell her what it means," he pleaded with me. "This is your law and I'm sure you learnt about creative diplomacy almost every day at varsity."

"I also have no idea what it means, bra PP," I said honestly, turning the meat on the braai.

"Okay, creative diplomacy means ukumokola," he said drunkenly.

A harsh cough followed and PP spat the phlegm on the ground. I watched him thrust his left hand into the pocket of his woven pants and come out with a blue handkerchief. He cleared his throat and spat again before dabbing his nose and the corners of his mouth.

"The way you're coughing, I think you should go for an HIV test," Mama joked.

"Over my dead body! I'll never go for that shit!" PP responded quickly.

"Why? Do you want to spread your Aids to your women?" Mama asked.

"Hey, I know I don't have that shit!"

"How do you know that, huh? Did you go for the test recently?" asked sis Zinhle sarcastically.

"Bullshit! The best way of testing yourself for HIV is to get your girlfriend pregnant. If her brat comes out clean, then you know that you're okay as well. All my kids are negative of the worms and that includes the new one whose maintenance case I'm attending in Durban."

"What if one comes out positive? What are you going to do then? Kill yourself?" asked sis Zinhle.

"What?" he said. "Me? Kill myself? Just look at me. This is Pele-pele, the real chilli. Ngishisa bhe! I'm very hot!"

PP's words and expression brought loud laughter from all of us. He boastfully hit his chest again and then pulled the brim of his hat down over his whole face and shouted, "Ngishisa bhe! I have my umbimbi. If I become positive with the worms I'll simply use it, but I doubt if I'll ever get that disease because I'm the real chilli."

"The way you boast about your tool, I'm telling you that one of these days you're going to get it. Aids is real!" said sis Zinhle, mixing her Amarula with ice cream.

At that moment I saw Vee arrive at the entrance to our dusty driveway. Her face was free of make-up and she looked very beautiful in her tight blue Levi jeans and white top. When Mama saw her she smiled.

"Here is my makoti. As you can see, my daughter-in-law is a beautiful lady inside and out. She's not like the cheap women that PP is talking about," said Mama as she went to greet Vee.

PP dismissed Mama's comment with a contemptuous wave of his hand.

"You must come to me for an hour's lesson on women, Advo," said PP, dropping his cigarette butt on the ground and extinguishing it with his heel. "They're capable of enriching your life or tearing it apart, especially if they are as beautiful as her."

Suddenly, Uncle Nyawana, who had been dozing in his chair, his head flopping drunkenly, woke up.

"If you stick with PP you'll inevitably get yourself into trouble, my Advo," he said in a slurred voice as if he were still asleep. "He's jealous of you because your girlfriend is hot like atchar."

"Nyawana is right, Advo. You must warn your girlfriend not to look at PP's ugly face when she helps us give food to these drunkards," said sis Zinhle, sounding as if she were conspiring against PP. "I heard that you can catch Aids just by looking at him."

We all burst into laughter, but PP struck a pose of bitter outrage; he was consumed with indignation.

"Shut up you, Zinhle!" snapped PP, his voice growing aggressive. "If I have Aids I was probably infected by you."

"In your horny dreams, of course," said sis Zinhle.

When I looked up again from the braai, Vee was already in the kitchen helping Mama stir the pap. Almost everyone was looking at her as she emerged from the kitchen carrying two plates. I watched PP's eyes picking at her legs before they landed on her breasts as she gave my uncle and Dilika their share of the food. Vee's wide, sexy mouth was stretched in a smile as she left the plates and went back to the kitchen. I looked at her beautiful legs and silently thanked nature for giving them to her.

There was silence as PP went to urinate in the corner of the yard behind Zero's zozo. On his way back from urinating he ignored the tap. He was talking even before he sat down in his chair.

"I think most of you don't know what you're talking about when you mention Aids," he said, pointing randomly at all of us, as Vee handed him his steaming pap. "For your information, you don't only get the worms through sex. I mean, in KwaZulu-Natal I have two Christian friends who swore to me that they never had sex in their lives, but now koloi ya Eliya is calling them. Yeah, they are dying of the damn worms." He blew on his hot pap.

"Liar! How's that possible?" asked Mama.

"It's a long story," he said, dipping his pap in the gravy, "but to cut a long story short, it happened differently for both of them."

"How?" insisted Mama, licking the gravy from her fingers.

"Oh, well, if you must know," PP said, swallowing his steaming pap, "one of them was lying naked and enjoying the sunset, like everyone else does, on Durban Beach. Then this naked bitch came running . . ." He demonstrated the woman running with his hands, the plate balanced on his knees. "She was a stripper from one of the beach-front brothels. I guess you all know that they have a lot of skin business there. Anyway, the bitch tripped, fell and landed right on the poor guy's horny dick. And then boom!" He swung his hands apart. "The poor guy was HIV positive."

We all laughed and even Vee seemed to be enjoying PP's story. She was sitting next to me on the plastic chair eating her pap. Behind Dilika on the trunk of the apricot tree I saw two lizards scurrying up and down, but no one noticed besides Vee and myself.

Sis Zinhle shrugged her shoulders and shook her head as PP threw a bone on the ground.

"You're a compulsive liar, PP!" she said as she watched Verwoerd eat the bone. "There's no way such a thing can happen. It's biologically impossible!"

"You're still young, Zinhle, and you know nothing. That's why I said that the story is long and complicated. I wanted to cut it very short. I mean the bitch had been sitting naked next to the poor guy all along. She could see that his joystick was getting interested in some action," he said, moving his forefinger slowly into an upright position, "and then she stood up and pretended to be running."

In the driveway I could see Zero parking his taxi just behind PP's BMW. He was playing kwaito music, "Minwana, phezulu" by Makhendlas, but he switched the engine off and got out of the taxi. He looked exhausted, as if he had been wrestling with a python, but he still greeted us before unlocking the door of his zozo and going inside.

"Well, PP, I don't believe you either," said Mama after responding to Zero's greeting.

"Okay, let me tell you about the other Christian that got the worms then. I told you they were two, didn't I?" he said, a toothpick dancing between his lips. "Okay, this lady was walking on the beach one afternoon when she stepped on a used syringe. You know there are crazy people in this world that don't want to die alone. So, somebody with HIV and a sick mind had deliberately put that syringe in the sand in a busy beach area. That's why I always avoid going to the beach . . ."

"You're a pathological liar!" said sis Zinhle.

"Read my lips! Bra PP is right," said Dilika, wiping away the whisky that was running down the sides of his mouth and onto his shirt. "I also know of a clinic here in Soweto where young, unemployed township people get tested after a weekend of unprotected sex in the hope that they are HIV positive," affirmed Dilika. "They know that if they are HIV positive they can apply for a state grant."

"Rubbish!" shouted sis Zinhle.

After an hour, the sky became grey as if it might rain. PP, Dilika and my uncle were all asleep in their chairs, with flies buzzing around their mouths. Verwoerd was busy licking a bone that my uncle still clutched in his hand, while an army of ants marched across the bones that were strewn all over the grass in front of PP and Dilika.

FOURTEEN
Sunday, December 26

"The only time to visit inmates at Sun City is at the weekend between seven in the morning and midday," Uncle Thulani said to me as he reversed his old yellow 1972 VW Beetle out of the paved driveway of his Naturena home. "And even then you can only see them for forty minutes."

It was already ten o'clock in the morning, but Sun City was easily within walking distance of Mama and Uncle Thulani's home and, if it hadn't been for Mama's pregnancy and Yuri's sickness, we could have walked there in less than twenty minutes. Mama was sitting with Uncle Thulani in the front of the Beetle and I was in the back with Yuri.

Uncle Thulani was wearing a pair of oversized brown trousers with sharp creases which he had fastened with a belt that had an oversized buckle. His polished black shoes shone like a mirror and his short-sleeved blue shirt was tucked nicely into his trousers. It had a small pocket on the left breast in which he had carefully placed his Parker pen.

Mama was wearing a wide-brimmed pink hat and her fingernails were painted pink as well. She was carrying her brown handbag and a white A4 envelope.

Between Yuri and me were two plastic bags full of food, cigarettes and other stuff for Uncle Guava. Yuri had already dirtied his brown shorts and red T-shirt with the yoghurt that he was eating. His gums looked inflamed around his straight white teeth. He was so frail, I thought, that the slightest wind would blow him away to the nearest cemetery.

"Idanyani is the worst place, Advo," said Uncle Thulani as the Beetle tried to negotiate the slope next to the Kaizer Chiefs Soccer Club Village. "You know, there's an old man there of more than sixty who earns R5 a month for cleaning the shoes of warders and other prisoners. He has been doing it for more than twenty years now."

"R5 per month?" Mama asked, scratching vigorously at her head. "I thought that I was the only one earning peanuts."

Uncle Thulani smiled and his fat cheeks grew bigger. He looked down at his brown lumber jacket that was resting on Mama's lap. It was excruciatingly hot and only Mama, Uncle Thulani and I knew why he had brought it along. He had concealed a bottle of my uncle's favourite KWV Premier Brandy under it and was going to give it to him as a belated Christmas gift from all of us. Uncle Thulani knew just how to smuggle the brandy into Sun City, as he had been working there as a warder for more than thirteen years. In fact, he and Mama had met a year and a half earlier during one of her regular visits to Uncle Guava.

"Like I said, Advo, this place is hell," emphasised Uncle Thulani as the old Beetle's engine emitted a cloud of foul, dark smoke. "Inside there you'll see an old man, kneeling down with his head bowed, addressing a young man as his father. Yeah, they call us vader and they respect us."

At the T-junction between the Johannesburg Prison and the shops, we came to a halt while Uncle Thulani surveyed the traffic. There were no robots there and seven or eight cars passed in front of us at high speed before the Beetle roared to the right, emitting more suffocating exhaust fumes.

Uncle Thulani indicated to the right, and the loud Beetle rolled towards the massive steel gates on which was written *Johannesburg Correctional Services*. He stopped at the gate, where floods of people were gushing in and out, and shared a boring joke with three of his uniformed colleagues. They were talking about Mama's pregnancy and how well Uncle Thulani had used his joystick on her. After signing a register, the boom gate opened and we drove towards a parking lot next to a grey building.

"On your right is the rehabilitation section," said Uncle Thulani as we climbed out of the Beetle, "and on your left is the juvenile section."

We walked between the large grey buildings, which to me looked more like warehouses where troublesome people like Uncle Guava were stored.

"Down here is the section for prisoners awaiting trial and behind it is the hospital section," added Uncle Thulani. "A little further up there is where we lock up the medium category of prisoners, who perform labour outside the prison, and that's where we're going."

As I followed Uncle Thulani, carrying the two plastic bags, I suddenly felt like a tourist in hell, being guided by the devil himself.

"I remember last year when one of the prisoners awaiting trial sold his new pair of All Star takkies for a cigarette. If you have a cigarette here in prison you instantly become a king. Your uncle, bra Guava, will be happy that he has four packets."

I smiled without humour and shifted the heavier plastic bag from one hand to the other.

"Thulani has been very good to your uncle, Bafana," Mama said, feeling Yuri's forehead with her left hand as he walked between us. "He had your uncle put into a single room."

Uncle Thulani was walking ahead of us now, with a confident swagger, his left hand in his pocket. After greeting some more warders he started talking again.

"Your uncle was in a communal cell with thirty-eight other prisoners before I got him a single cell," said Uncle Thulani, sounding like a man with power over life and death. "They shared four toilet rolls and one bar of soap which we replaced every two weeks."

"You have done a lot for him," I said finally.

Uncle Thulani didn't look at me or comment on my praise. Instead, he hitched his oversized trousers up over his belly and pointed at another grey building as if he were a tourist guide.

"That's the school section," he said, "and next to it is the maximum sentences section."

We entered a hall with high ceilings where a few prisoners in orange uniforms were busy talking to their visitors. Uncle Thulani asked us to sit on a long bench while he went away to call my uncle out. He was carrying his brown lumber jacket that concealed the brandy.

Uncle Guava was classified as a Category A prisoner, which meant that he was one of the lucky inmates who was entitled to forty-eight visits per year. I didn't know if this privilege was due to the fact that he had been in prison since 1997, or whether it was because of his good behaviour, but somehow I suspected that it all had something to do with Mama's relationship with Uncle Thulani.

"Your uncle will be very happy to see you," Mama said, stroking

Yuri, whose mouth immediately opened in a giant yawn. "He has been asking Thulani to pass on the message that you must come and visit him."

Yuri's face was still buried in the warmth of Mama's chest when Uncle Guava and Uncle Thulani appeared at the door. The last time I had visited my uncle in jail was in June, during the university vacation, and he had changed a lot since then. He came to prison as a tall, lean, bad-tempered person, but now he had thick hands, a broad chest and long, stout arms. He came towards me with his arms outstretched.

"I'm glad you came, Bafana," he said, hugging me before sitting down on the bench.

He still called me by my real name and it was obvious that he wasn't aware that I had earned myself a new nickname in the township. No one in my family besides him pronounced the letter B in my name as hard, yet with such fatherly tenderness.

"When Javas, PP and Dilika were here three weeks ago they brought me a phone card, but I haven't used it because the public phones in this hell are always out of order," he continued, as if he were looking for a sympathetic ear. "It's actually about two months now that they are not working."

Uncle Thulani excused himself while he went outside, probably to smoke. All the time I had been looking at my uncle, noticing how the prison had changed him. His voice had become soft and I guessed it was due to fatigue, inactivity and the monotonous routine of his days inside those intimidating grey structures.

"We brought you something," Mama said, pointing at the two plastic bags I had carried from the car.

My uncle Guava's eyes left mine reluctantly as he wiped his hands before digging inside the plastic bag for a cold pie. Yuri shot him an amused look as he chewed and swallowed loudly. He ate the pie ravenously, in three bites. As he wiped his mouth on the back of his hand, Mama whispered in his ear, as if to safeguard her deepest secret. My uncle's face glistened with delight as he counted the four packets of cigarettes inside the plastic bags.

"Thulani has also brought your favourite ugologo, buti, and it's with him. He'll give it to you later," she said to him.

"Ta, sester. He has given it to me already," he said without glancing at Mama. Instead, he turned to me and said, "Your ouledi has a nice person in bra Thuks, my laaitie. He's very kind. He gave me his old black-and-white TV and he even lends me a cellphone now and then, when I want to call your ouledi for help." The smile immediately vanished from his face. "I owe them a lot. Without them this prison would've been hell."

There was a moment of silence as if we were all running out of words, but before it became uncomfortable Yuri exploded into a fit of coughing. I expected my uncle to comment on his health, but he simply watched him critically without a word until Yuri stopped coughing.

"Your ouledi told me that you have a Zim girl, my laaitie. What's her name again?"

"Vee," said Mama, before I could answer.

"You must stick to her, Bafana. Who knows, maybe President Mugabe will reward you for strengthening diplomatic ties with one of those expropriated farms. I'll come to work for you two and start a new life in that beautiful country," he concluded, trying to smile.

"No, she's not my girlfriend, Uncle," I responded, shaking my head, "she's just a friend that I met esgele."

"Ja, talking about sgele, Rea tells me that you can't have your results," he said with concern in his voice.

"That's the other reason that we've come to see you," said Mama before he could ask another question. "We desperately need your help."

"For these two years you've been very helpful to me, sester. If it's within my power, I will help."

"This is very hard for me," said Mama, looking away, "but I was thinking that we could sell the house to raise the funds for Bafana."

Uncle Guava bit his lip and tried to lock eyes with Mama, but she outstared him and he ended up looking away. I already had enough guilt of my own to deal with and I had actually hoped that Mama wouldn't bring up the idea of selling the house.

"Sell the house?" he finally said, looking down at his feet.

"Well . . . I know this is hard for all of us, but I was thinking that since you have an RDP house in Slovoville we could come to a compromise. I mean, that's if it's fine with you," she said, black-mailing him into agreement.

"I see. Have you talked to Javas about this?" said Uncle Guava, referring to Uncle Nyawana by his tsotsi name again.

"Not yet," Mama lied. "I thought I should talk to you first as you are the eldest in the family."

"I understand," he said, giving Mama three rapid nods. "So, how do we go about this?"

Mama opened the white A4 envelope that she had brought with her and handed the contents to my uncle.

"I've been speaking to a lawyer just in case. He drafted me this letter of consent and all you need to do is sign," she said.

Uncle Guava scanned the letter and signed it with the pen that Mama gave him. As he did so, I noticed Uncle Thulani standing at the door. He was pointing at his watch, indicating that visiting time was up. Uncle Guava stood up first and shook Mama's hand before bundling Yuri and me together in one big hug.

"You must come visit me often, Bafana," said my uncle, his voice giving away his sadness.

"I'll come next week with your Kuveve brandy, Uncle," I said, joking to quell my guilt, but to my uncle it must have sounded like a genuine promise.

FIFTEEN
Friday, December 31

It was still only nine o'clock in the evening, but there was already great excitement in our street. Most of us kept glancing at our watches in anticipation of the special New Year to come. In just a few hours we would be entering the new millennium. No one, including small kids, was prepared to miss the excitement and drama that always accompanied the New Year by falling asleep.

"Bafana, please fetch me the sponge from under your bed," asked Mama. "Yuri has to sleep outside so he can see the first day of the new millennium. We'll wake him up at twelve exactly. He can't sleep in there, it's too hot," she said, pointing at the house.

I went inside my room where Yuri was sleeping on another sponge that Mama had spread on the floor. His mouth was open and his thin hands had been bitten by the mosquitoes that were buzzing angrily in the room. Sleeping on my bed was sis Zinhle's daughter, Mbali. I fished underneath my bed and came out with a sponge.

"He has made it already, chomza," declared sis Zinhle as I brought the sponge outside and Mama entered the house to fetch Yuri. "Most people thought he was going to die long before the millennium, and look!"

Mama came out with Yuri. She laid him down on the sponge and immediately covered him with three blankets to prevent him from getting a fever. After doing that, Mama suggested that we should all close our eyes, kneel down and pray. Praying was a strange rite to me, but I agreed, while Uncle Nyawana, Dilika, Zero and PP refused.

Mama ignored my uncle and his drunken friends and started to pray for us while we all held hands, but my uncle and his friends didn't stop talking while Mama was praying and I heard them arguing.

"Why should I pray?" said Uncle Nyawana. "I mean, God already knows all my problems and if He's willing to help let Him come forward."

"Bra Nyawana, do you expect God to come and find you?" Zero asked when our eyes were closed in prayer.

"I have my pride. If He's willing to help, He knows where to find me, I'm not hiding like He is," my uncle replied.

As we opened our eyes I heard some singing coming from the direction of Priest Mthembu's house. Nosily, I went to the fence to see who was singing, but all I could see was a group of people standing right in the middle of the street, singing and dancing to a popular hymn.

Linamandla, linamandla,	(It's powerful, it's powerful, it's
linamandla igazi lemvana.	powerful, the blood of the Lamb.)
Lisusa zonk'izono.	(It removes all the sins.)

Priest Mthembu had told us that Jesus would come at twelve on the dot to destroy the sinners. That thought made me a bit nervous as it was obvious that I would miss Jesus's bus to heaven because of the lies I had told to my family and my secret drinking and smoking.

I left the fence and came back to sit on my chair next to Zero.

"Who are those people singing out so loud, Advo?" asked my uncle as I sat down.

"They're the church people at the corner there by maMfundisi's house."

"Somebody must tell them that today is not the day to be serious. They must put a smile on their faces because we're approaching the millennium," responded my uncle.

* * *

As the night slowly descended on us, Uncle Nyawana's dog, Verwoerd, started to yap and squeak as massive firecracker after massive firecracker exploded in the sky above us. Eventually, he crawled between my uncle's leg and stump for protection.

"Bafana, please go and wake my daughter," asked sis Zinhle. "It's almost time now and I don't want her to miss the millennium."

It seemed I was there only to run everybody's errands and I hated it, but I did as I was asked. I stepped inside my room where Mbali was sleeping on my single bed, with her knees pulled up under her chin. She was fourteen years old and beautiful like her mother.

"Wakey wakey, Mbali, it's the millennium already!" I said, shaking her gently while she slept.

Mbali blinked her eyes open and rubbed them. Slowly she rolled over and stared at me. She looked more skeleton than flesh, as her ambition was to be a model and an actress. Her face was all jaw and eye socket and, when she walked, her arms looked brittle and twig-like.

PP flashed his bad teeth as we came out of the house together.

"Dudlu!" he sang. "Khula sihlahla sizodla'mapentshisi!"

Embarrassed, Mbali looked away while her mother tried to protect her.

"Leave my daughter alone, you ugly paedophile monkey! Can't you see you're scaring her? Do you want her to have nightmares?"

"Who are you calling ugly?" asked PP.

"You! Can't you see you're as black as Africa itself! I think that when God made you He was only joking. Look at your nose! It's so huge! It's as if God ran out of human organs and threw that oversized one at your ugly black face from His old wardrobe of animal organs."

PP touched his nose gently with his hand.

"Having a big nose means nothing. As long as young women like her love it, it's fine with me. Look at your daughter, she loves it. Is it not romantic, girl, huh?" responded PP.

Mbali smiled and fastened her hair with a leather thong while PP sucked in smoke from his zol.

"Look, she's smiling!" he continued. "That means she'll marry me because I'm handsome in her eyes. Can't you see that it's this nose that charms your beautiful daughter?"

"Haibo! Sies! The person that'll marry my daughter will have to be rich and famous with at least a six-digit salary a month. It won't be a loser like you who robs and kills people to survive. My future son-in-law must be prepared to pay fifty cows for my daughter's lobola, and all of those cows must be pregnant," said sis Zinhle boastfully.

"That's not a bad demand at all for rich people like us. I can afford that myself," said PP, hitting his chest. "Leave Mbali with me for a day and I'll take care of her."

"What? You think I'm stupid, huh? Only a fool would ask a leopard to look after a springbok."

Dilika passed a zol to Uncle Nyawana.

"Ahhhh! This is good shit!" my uncle whispered after a few puffs. "I think that you guys must shut up about your lobola shit. What's the use of paying fifty pregnant cows just to marry one useless nagging cow?"

"Dream on, Jabu!" Mama said scornfully. "That's the reason my sister-in-law, Dudu, left you."

"Aarg, the only reason that Dudu has left me is because I bought her shoes," said my uncle. Then he turned to me and said, "Advo, my laaitie, you must never buy your Vee shoes as a gift. If you do, she'll leave you and go home to Zimbabwe. Yeah, she'll disappoint you and walk away to other men while wearing the shoes that you bought for her."

With difficulty my uncle tried to stand up, but he was too drunk. Before he fell down I quickly gave him some support. He took his crutches, which he had left leaning against the wall, and limped inside the house.

"Where are you going now? To sleep?" asked sis Zinhle.

"Haibo! Why should I report to you where I'm going? I'm going to six nine in the toilet and if you want to hold my four five while I stand and pee you're most welcome to do so, Zinhle," he said, laughing.

"Sies! I wonder if you still have that four five left on you."

Within seconds my uncle was back with the new bottle of J&B whisky that Mama had bought for him during the day, as well as the three big firecrackers that I had bought to contribute to the celebrations with part of the R150 that I had stolen from Mama's stokvel money.

"It's time to stop talking and to start celebrating," he said, opening the bottle.

* * *

At exactly twelve midnight the street was full of people and most of them were dancing excitedly to the kwaito song that came from the Jobe's place. It was one of the hottest songs of the moment, one by Mdu called "Mazola".

Baba kaNomsa.	(Nomsa's father.)
Gibela phezu'kwendlu.	(Climb to the rooftop.)
Ubatshele, uMazolo sekadaar.	(Tell them Mazola is here.)

The whole of Soweto had been reduced to one big party. I watched as my uncle took off his favourite UCT T-shirt and, in the heat of the moment, climbed excitedly onto the wall that separated us from our neighbours. That entertained everyone because the wall was quite high for a one-legged person like him. He was drunk, but he effortlessly hopped just once and then stood with his one leg on the wall. In his right hand he was carrying a bottle of whisky and in his left he carried one of the firecrackers that I had bought earlier in the day. His trousers were loose around his waist, exposing his underpants.

Encouraged by the crowd, he moved his stump back and forth with astonishing vigour, and, as if that were not enough, he held up his open bottle of whisky and shouted, "Let me show you how to drink alcohol! If I quit drinking, thousands of people will be retrenched at South African Breweries."

My cellphone beeped twice. I had received my first message of the new millennium. It was from Vee and I started reading it as some kids gave my uncle a box of matches that he immediately used to light the firecracker, which he pointed at the sky.

May our relationship never sink as low as my bank balance, but grow as strong as black people's love for free things.

Suddenly, there was a bang, followed by a scream and the smell of burning flesh. I looked up at the wall where my uncle had been dancing, but he was no longer there. He had fallen next to the stump of the peach tree.

"Nkosi yam! Please don't let him die," Mama screamed as she ran towards him. She fell next to him on her knees as if she were praying. "Please, Jabu, you owe that life of yours to us!" she wailed, looking around for help.

SIXTEEN
Wednesday, January 5, 2000

It was a few days after my uncle's accident. The millennium had come and gone and Jesus had stood Soweto up. The computers at the banks hadn't crashed either, but my uncle was still in hospital. That morning when Mama came back from work she passed by Chi to see me. I had just bathed and was still in my boxers and my fur-lined slippers when she called me into the kitchen. She sounded a bit happier and, as she had been to the hospital to see my uncle, I thought that she must have good news.

"You know what, baby?" started Mama. "I was at the hospital today and Zinhle introduced me to Dr Malambe, her friend."

"How is my uncle doing?" I asked. "Is his condition improving?"

"No, it's still the same, but Dr Malambe has agreed to sign the letter for the sale of the house on behalf of your uncle as he has no legal capacity."

"But, Mama, how can we do this without his real consent?"

"What do you mean? I'm doing this for you."

"Okay," I said reluctantly.

"And the good news is that Zinhle has agreed to lend me R20 000 so long. I'll repay her when the sale of the house has gone through."

"But, Mama, that was unnecessary. I'm going to get a job and pay the university myself. You can use the money to renovate the house in Naturena."

"Are you out of your mind, Bafana? All this work and you want to withdraw now? How can you get a job without qualifications?

There is no way, not here in Mzansi anyway. Come on, we'll take the money, and if you feel like paying it back after making your millions you can do so."

Mama left me R500 to book my bus ticket to Cape Town with. I walked her to the end of our gateless driveway where Uncle Thulani's Beetle was already roaring. After greeting Uncle Thulani, I called Zero from my cellphone to find out if he was anywhere near Chi. I was in luck, he was in Protea and on his way to the city.

I changed into my layered golf T-shirt, Nike trainers and brown cargo pants, and walked to the Mangalani BP Garage on the Old Potchefstroom Road. While waiting for Zero there, my phone rang, and it was Yomi.

"Ke ije, umunne? How is it going, brother? It's Yomi from Yeoville Internet Café, do you remember me? We talked about opening the internet café business in Soweto the other day, remember?"

"Oh yes, Yomi, I remember you."

"I want us to meet and discuss how to start it, my brother."

"When do you want us to meet?"

"How is your schedule today? I'm free, you can come any time."

"Okay, I'll come around one."

"See you then."

"Sharp."

By half past eleven I was already inside Zero's taxi, but the traffic was moving slowly. Bunju was sitting just behind the driver's seat. She was wearing ice-wash jeans, short black boots and a brown poloneck. As the taxi passed the Moroka Police Station along the Old Potchefstroom Road, I noticed Zero staring at a luxury silver Audi A3 in the other lane.

"That's what I have a problem with, Advo," he said, shaking his head as if he were grossly disappointed. "You see what Tata Mandela and President Mbeki have done to us black men? This crazy system of theirs means that young black women drive expensive cars while we black men still belong to the walking class."

"Don't be jealous, man! The opportunities are there for everyone. We just have to work a little harder," I said.

Zero shook his head and looked at me without saying a word. I thought he had finished talking about the woman and her Audi, but I soon realised that he was just searching for more words. As we passed the Regina Mundi, the largest Catholic church in Soweto, the Audi was cruising at the same speed as Zero's taxi. He glanced at it again and whistled.

"Just look at her, Advo! She has such a sense of self-importance. That's why most young Mzansi women today are UDFs. Unmarried, Divorced or Frustrated. I tell you, Advo, these women's chances of finding Mr Right are almost nonexistent here in Mzansi," he said as we passed the railway bridge that separates Kliptown and Pimville. "You might be educated, Advo," he continued, his dark, unshaven face turning to stare at me, "but you don't have the experience that I have. Siriyasi, I tell you, Advo! These rich black women are more likely to be bitten by a big shark in their big swimming pools than find the right man."

We all laughed, even Bunju and the people sitting just behind us.

"But no shark can live in a swimming pool, man, sharks only live in the ocean," I said, stating the obvious.

"That's my point, Advo! If no shark can live in a swimming pool, then there's no right man here in Mzansi."

126

He looked at his wing mirror, shifted gear and overtook a blue car by the Diepkloof Hostel next to Bara Hospital. I could hear the taxi's tyres running over the cat's-eyes on the edge of the freeway as we passed another car. The woman sitting between Zero and myself shouted "Southgate" just before the N12 off-ramp to Witbank.

As we passed South African Breweries on our way to Southgate, I saw the Audi indicating to the right in the direction of Sun City. Zero stared at it and I read his face curiously. "We're all crooks here in Mzansi, man! Politicians, hawkers, businesspeople, government workers, police, traffic cops, lawyers, prostitutes, all of us, Advo," said Zero, still staring after the car. "We're all crooks, including these successful young women. The majority of them fuck their way up the corridors of power."

"I don't believe that!"

"Siriyasi, Advo, I know so," he insisted. "And you know another reason why these successful women can't find the right man?" he asked, concentrating on the road.

"Why?"

"It's because they only open their mouths to speak to men that earn more than twenty grand per month," he said, with unhidden anger. "But once they realise that those special men they're looking for are taken, they become frustrated and end up joining this new secret society, MADS."

"MADS? What's that?" I asked.

"You don't know what MADS is? That's because you have not been married, Advo. I was married once, to my childhood sweetheart."

"You were married before?"

"Siriyasi. There's a lot you don't know about me, Advo. I'm also a first-year dropout from Fort Hare University."

"Wow, what did you do there?"

"Social Sciences, but I was dismissed because of politics in the late eighties."

"Is that so?"

"Siriyasi, Advo, and my woman left me because I didn't benefit from those same politics like all the other crooks."

I realised for the first time that Zero was a stranger to me.

"Siriyasi, Advo, my sweetheart is now married to a famous politician."

"Sorry to hear that."

"Don't worry, because she's not happy with him. That's why she joined the MADS again. She called me the other day and told me that she wants to divorce him."

"So, what's this MADS thing?" I asked again.

"Oh, that's the Men Are Dogs Society. Haven't you heard about it, Advo?"

"No, I haven't."

"MADS is the secret society for unhappy black women here in Jo'burg, Advo. They sometimes call themselves ABC or Angry Black Chicks. They regularly meet at gyms and restaurants, in malls like Rosebank, where they plot how they can manipulate their men while drinking expensive whiskies and smoking cigars. And you know what they call black men like me and you? They call us The Beasts of the Y-Chromosome."

"You're talking bull," I said, laughing at Zero's serious face.

"Siriyasi. What I'm saying is true, Advo. At least you have a bright future, but I'm only a damned taxi driver for the rest of my life. Unless I hijack a nice G-string BMW, these women will always look down upon the likes of me."

"Try this new lotto, my bra. You might win the four million rand jackpot."

He looked at me as if I had just insulted him.

"Shit! Fuck that robbing game. You'll never win. You'll never even get three consolation numbers. It's just a waste of hard-earned zak. A good example is bra Nyawana. He gambles on fah-fee almost every day. Look where he is now, in Bara Hospital, and he never won that shit."

"So, you don't believe in lotto?"

"Hell no, have you ever come across a person that has won the lotto? Look at the queues for the lotto in Chi. You want to tell me that all the people are playing the wrong numbers?"

"Well, I haven't come across a person that's won it, but that doesn't mean that people don't win . . ."

"I tell you, Advo, that lotto is a form of Black Economic Enrichment. Tata ma chance, loser ma millions. Siriyasi, how do you think politicians like Seroka and Mabizela got rich? Have you seen Mabizela's old four-roomed township home in Chi? Well, now he owns a mansion, there in Bassonia." He pointed randomly at the suburb at the top of the hill next to Southgate. "Where do you think all the money comes from? It comes from the lotto, of course."

"Is that right?"

"Siriyasi, Advo. The lotto is just a clever money-laundering scheme. It was designed by the rich black politicians and now they are just helping each other to get rich with it," he said loudly.

Most people laughed, including Bunju, and Zero looked at her in the rear-view mirror.

"Siriyasi, 'strue 'sgod," he swore. "The politicians are busy exploiting the minds of poor people to enrich themselves. By the time they spin that wheel they already know who the winner is. Why do you think that there are a lot of wealthy black families, huh? They all got their money from the lotto. They're all crooks."

"Serious?"

He engaged the gear.

"Siriyasi, Advo. The first Saturday a father of one of the politicians will win, and the following week it'll be the daughter of the same politician and then the son, and so on and so on. But you and I? Forget it, Advo," he shook his head, "we'll never win. I'm telling you, Advo, 'strue 'sgod." He kissed his hand and pointed it at the roof of his taxi. "These politicians are all crooks, they learnt it in exile."

I looked out of the side window and smiled to myself.

"Do you want to prove that this world belongs to the politicians, Advo?" asked Zero, glancing at me. "Just steal R20 from anyone inside this taxi and you'll spend fifteen to twenty years in prison with hard labour, but let the politician steal twenty million rand of poor taxpayers' money and you'll see. They always get away with it. Where's the justice, Advo, tell me? There is no justice. There's just us. You and me, Advo."

At Southgate Mall the lady sitting between us got out of the taxi.

"My Bunjubunju," Zero called out. "Come and join us up here in the front, my baby."

I immediately jumped out so that Bunju could sit in the middle between us.

"Ah, today I can feel your blood running fast in your veins, my sweetheart," Zero began as the taxi sped off to join the M1 freeway to the city. "Siriyasi, I can feel it circulating smoothly in your body, baby, and that's because you're sitting between two important men. Advo is from the High Court, the highest place, where great laws are made," he added unnecessarily as he changed gear.

Bunju smiled and looked at me.

"I know that, Zero, but who's the other important person you're talking about?" she asked sarcastically.

"Of course, the other person is me, myself and I. I need no introduction to you because I know you always dream of me."

Bunju flashed a huge smile.

"Well, perhaps I think of you sometimes, but I don't dream of you."

"What's the difference, my Bunju? Thinking and dreaming are both the same, isn't it, Advo?" he asked as another car sped past us.

Before I could answer, Zero shifted his attention back to Bunju.

"Thinking of me is like dreaming of me with your eyes open, sweetie-pie. Can you see now that the difference between the two is separated by the thickness of a hair, huh? Tell her, Advo!"

I smiled without saying a word. By Gold Reef Casino Zero indicated to the left and joined Booysens Road.

"Remember I told you some time back that I'd get my advocate friend to help you to apply for your child grant?"

"Oh, yes, I remember," Bunju said with a lot of interest in her voice.

"Well, you're sitting next to him right now, baby," he said, nodding his head.

Bunju smiled again. She also thought that I was an advocate, as the delicious whisperings were following me everywhere.

"I know that Advo is an advocate," Bunju said.

"So, if you know, don't just sit there; you must set an appointment with him. You have to fix everything as soon as possible," he said. "Time is money, sweetheart."

* * *

I got out of Zero's taxi at the corner of Bree and Rissik Streets and walked to Park Station. It was buzzing with people and there was heavy luggage all over the concourse. There were also long queues at all of the bus company counters, but I managed to get a Greyhound ticket for the following Tuesday.

After booking my ticket I went to Yeoville to check my e-mail. I arrived there at about half past two in the afternoon. Unlike the previous time when I had been there, most of the computers were unoccupied. Yomi was there waiting for me. Before we spoke business, he logged me onto a computer for free. I had seven new messages in my inbox. Two of them were from Vee and the rest were from people I didn't know.

As soon as I had logged myself off, Yomi and I had a chat about setting up an internet café in Chi. After that I called Mama from the public telephone in the internet café and told her that I had booked a bus for Tuesday evening. We agreed that I would sleep in Naturena on Monday as it would be easier for me to get to Park Station and, from there, to Cape Town.

SEVENTEEN
Tuesday, January 11

In my room in Naturena, I packed the clothes that I had just ironed into my sports bag. Mama had already gone to work, but she had left me a brown envelope with R22 000 in cash on the kitchen table. It was the first time that I had ever had such a large sum of money on me.

I said goodbye to Yuri and Aunty Manto, the lady that helped Mama look after him, and made my way out into the street. My plan was to kill time by meeting Yomi at his internet café in Yeoville and discussing his business plan. After that I thought I might as well go to Johannesburg Magistrate's Court to listen to some cases.

There was no free ride from Zero this time, as Naturena wasn't on his taxi route, so I took a different taxi from near Sun City into the city. The silence inside the taxi removed me from reality and my uncle's face began to weave in and out of my mind.

As I thought about my uncle I suddenly became very tense. I realised that I had set myself a trap. There I was, in that taxi, stuck with the cash that I was supposed to pay for my nonexistent results. What was I going to do with it now? I asked myself.

I was busy tossing around two options in my mind as the taxi passed Southgate Mall. The first one was to stay with a friend in Cape Town until I found a job. I could probably cook up a story to fool Mama. I'd tell her that I had joined a well-established law firm in Cape Town. Mama would be disappointed, of course, but she would surely understand. The other option was to go back to UCT and beg to be readmitted.

I reached Yeoville at about ten o'clock in the morning. Somehow the heat seemed to be slowing time down.

After talking about opening an internet café at the Mangalani BP Garage, Yomi started to ask me uncomfortable questions about my trip to Cape Town.

"You say you're going to Cape Town today? I didn't know that you had a degree in law," he said.

"Well, there's a problem, man, because I owe the varsity lots of money, about twenty grand. I'm just going to negotiate with them to give me my results, but I doubt if they'll let me have them."

"My brother, I know these varsities and I doubt too if you'll get your results. That's the reason we must work hard together in Soweto. We can make a hell of a lot of money. When are you coming back?" Yomi asked.

"I'm not sure, man, it might take longer than I think."

Yomi looked a bit disappointed, but then, out of the blue, my new-found Nigerian friend said, "Oh, I see. I can help you with that, my brother, by hooking you up with my guys."

"What?"

"Yeah, I know a guy that sells certificates, man. Even big guys in big companies have bought from him, man. This is Africa, my friend."

"I don't think I want to buy a certificate."

"Don't be shy, my brother. Come back to me when you think you're ready."

"Please don't tell Vee that we had this conversation," I begged.

134

I left Yomi's place deep in thought, but deep down I knew he had convinced me. I told myself that I had to do something to escape the perpetual misery of my existence in the township.

Instead of going to Park Station to catch the bus to Cape Town, I caught a taxi from Yeoville to Bramley where I found a B&B. I took a room, for R300 a day, at the Carta Novo on the corner of Corlett Drive and Louis Botha Avenue. I knew that Bramley wasn't Mama's kind of place. There was no way she would find out that I was hiding there.

That night I called Yomi again and he asked me to give him my full names as they appeared in my ID. I did that and he promised to call me the following day. Later, I also called Mama and lied to her, telling her that I was safely on my way to Cape Town. She had been to the hospital to see my uncle during the day.

"How is Uncle doing at the hospital?" I asked.

"His condition is getting worse every day. He hasn't improved at all."

"Did they tell you why?"

"The doctor says that it's because of respiratory complications. I don't think he'll live much longer."

"What makes you say that, Mama? We mustn't lose hope."

"I mean, there's no longer a human being there. You'll see for yourself when you come back."

EIGHTEEN
Wednesday, January 12

The morning of the following day, Yomi called to say that my degree was ready. In the back room of his internet café I collected the document that was printed with the words:

AT A CONGREGATION OF THE UNIVERSITY HELD ON THE 12TH OF JANUARY 2000, BAFANA KUZWAYO WAS ADMITTED TO BACHELOR OF LAWS.

The certificate was so convincing that I was sure that discovery was out of the question. Even the vice-chancellor himself would not have been able to tell that his signature wasn't genuine. There was also the University of Cape Town's Spes Bona logo on it.

I paid R2 000 for the certificate and my statement of results. I had received very high marks in all the courses that I had failed dismally.

In the afternoon I went to Balfour Park Mall's Absa Bank to deposit R18 000 of the R19 600 that was left of Mama's money. When I had finished in the bank I walked to Ultra City Liquors on the corner of Louis Botha Avenue and Corlett Drive and bought myself a bottle of J&B. Then I went to my room to drink. I had just under R1 000 in my pocket.

After drinking a few glasses of whisky alone in my room I decided to call Mama from my cellphone.

"Hello, baby, did you go well?" she asked.

"I went well, Mama," I said, trying hard to sound sober. "I even got my results today."

"That's my boy! And I'm sure you've done well."

"I did very well, Mama. You'll see when I come back."

"You're still coming tomorrow, aren't you, baby?"

"Yeah, I've booked the bus already. I'll be on it later this afternoon."

"You must come tomorrow, I've arranged for us all to go to the hospital on Friday. You must see your uncle before he passes away."

"Don't say that, Mama. I'll see you on Friday."

That night I drank until I blacked out.

NINETEEN
Thursday, January 13

It took several loud knocks on my door for Ms Zitha, the B&B owner, to get my attention. I looked at the time on my cellphone and
realised that it was already half past ten in the morning. I should
have checked out of the room thirty minutes earlier.

With the five minutes Ms Zitha gave me to check out of the room,
I quickly brushed my teeth and washed my face. Ten minutes later
I signed out and handed the key to Ms Zitha, whose make-up looked
like red mud that had been smeared across her face.

I didn't want to go home before the time the bus was due to arrive at Park Station. I had to kill time until at least half past twelve
in the afternoon. As I walked out of the gate I was already planning
on treating myself to a nice breakfast at Balfour Park Mall's Mugg
& Bean. At least money wasn't an issue any more.

I walked along Corlett Drive towards Louis Botha Avenue, where
I took an Alexandra-bound taxi. It only took five minutes to reach
the mall. Although this was not the kind of place Mama, sis Zinhle
or Nina would come shopping, I had to be careful because it was
the kind of place Vee would come to shop. Just to make sure that
she wasn't around, I decided to call her.

"Hi, Vee, it's Bee here. Where are you?" I asked, as I walked into
CNA to buy the *Sowetan* and *The Star*.

"Hi, Bee, are you back from Cape Town already?"

"I'm on my way back."

"Okay. Where are you?"

"We're approaching Vereeniging, and where are you?"

"I'm here at work. I'm knocking off late tonight," she said, as I tendered a R10 note at the till.

"Okay, great. I just wanted to tell you how excited I am. I got my results!"

"Congratulations! That's very good news! I'd love to meet you to celebrate, but we're having a farewell party here at the hospital. One of our members is leaving for Britain. She got a good nursing job there. Hey, why don't you come? I know that you'll be tired, but . . ."

"When's the party?" I asked as I took the change and walked out of the store towards Mugg & Bean.

"It's at four this afternoon. Just come to the reception area and ask for the conference room. They'll let you in."

"Well, okay, I'll see if I can make it."

"I can ask one of my friends to fetch you at Park Station if you want."

"No. Don't worry about it."

I sat down in the corner of Mugg & Bean with my cap drawn down over my eyes to avoid the gaze of anyone who might recognise me. As soon as the waitress came I ordered bacon and eggs with four slices of toasted bread. I chewed the food slowly and without pleasure as I browsed through the newspapers. When I had finished my breakfast I called the waitress and ordered a double J&B on the rocks. I stayed at the Mugg & Bean until three o'clock in the afternoon. I had been there since half past eleven and the bill was almost R300. I had had a lot of whisky.

At about quarter to four the meter taxi that I had caught just outside the mall was cruising along Empire Road, next to Wits, in the direction of Milpark Hospital. We came to a stop in a tree-lined street next to the hospital gate, where I handed the driver R200 before he left.

I looked at the sign on my left, next to the security gates. It was written in three languages, English, Afrikaans and Zulu:

NO VACANCY

GEEN WERK

AWUKHO UMSEBENZI

On my right I saw an arrow pointing to the left for the reception. Next to that was another sign that was also written in English, Afrikaans and Zulu and it said:

NO HAWKERS ALLOWED

GEEN SMOUSE

UKUTHENGISA AKUVUNYELWA

The security guard at the gate gave me a pen and register book in which to print my name and that of the person I was going to visit. After I had finished I walked towards reception.

"How may I help you, sir?" asked the lady at the reception desk.

"I've come to see Vimbai Mataruse," I answered, trying hard not to look drunk.

"You must be Bafana, right? Follow the passage and then turn right where the arrow points to the conference room. That's where Vee is. You won't miss it," she said.

I sneaked into the conference room where a small crowd was standing and listening to a tall lady talk. I saw Vee on the other side of the room and she smiled at me. The rest of the people were facing the tall lady, who spent the next fifteen minutes telling the staff how much they were all going to miss the lady that was leaving. I listened without interest; my mind was on the food and the bottles of wine I had spotted on the table at the back of the room.

"Congratulations again! How was Cape Town?" asked Vee as I made my way over to her after the speeches had ended.

"Boring!" I lied. "The students haven't arrived yet. There were just a few people there for the supplementary exams."

"Any news about your uncle?"

"I called Mama yesterday and she says that he's getting worse."

"I'm sorry about that," she said as I took a glass of red wine from the table.

"Yeah, they say he's got respiratory complications," I said, taking a gulp from my glass.

"That's what I hate about public hospitals. I'm sure if he was in a private hospital like this he would be fine by now. We have the best doctors here!" she declared.

At that moment, Vee's cellphone rang and, because of the noise in the conference room, she went outside to answer it. That gave me an opportunity to visit the table with the food again and, with no one paying attention, I stuffed a slice of cheese into my pocket. I cut another big slice of cheese, threw it into my mouth and then quickly swallowed two glasses of red wine. I then looked around again and, when no one was looking, pocketed three muffins, two chicken wings and some samoosas. By the time Vee came back I already had another glass of red wine in my hand. I was feeling quite drunk.

* * *

The party ended at about half past seven. I left Vee at the hospital and went to catch a taxi on Empire Road to Bree Street, and from there another one to Soweto.

By the time the taxi joined the M1 South I was already asleep in my seat. All the windows were shut to avoid the wind, but as the taxi sped along the smell of petrol became overwhelming and I started to suffocate. At the same time my bladder was pressing me and I badly needed to urinate. Suddenly, I was seized by a terrible need to vomit and, as we passed Southgate Mall on the road to Bara Hospital, I could no longer control my gut.

A nurse, wearing her Bara Hospital uniform, was sitting right in front of me. I made a desperate vomiting motion and as she turned her face and looked towards the back, the vomit came straight out of my mouth. Three great heaves from my gut landed on her. I could see small balls of undigested cheese stuck on her uniform and plaited hair.

"Uhhhh, I'm sorry, sister. I'm not feeling well," I managed to mutter in a conciliatory tone.

"Voetsek! Your mother must have been made pregnant by a pig to produce a useless shit like you!" cursed the lady sitting next to the nurse. My puke had landed on the shoulder of her white jacket, staining it pink. "Why didn't you sit by the window if you felt sick?" she continued.

"Sorry, I didn't think . . ."

"Sies, you're a pig. You're not sick, you are just drunk."

I realised that I had also vomited on the pants of the guy that was sitting next to me, but the taxi driver was the next one to confront me.

"Who threw up in my taxi?" he asked in a dangerous tone of voice.

"It's this stupid monkey here at the back," said the guy next to me.

"You'll wash my taxi tonight and not tomorrow!" said the taxi driver, and I noticed the deep scarifications on his face as he spoke.

"You must first wash my trousers and then come and explain to my wife what happened," said the guy next to me. "My wife can't touch some godforsaken drunkard's vomit."

"But it wasn't on purpose, sir," I said, avoiding eye contact.

"I don't care. You must come and say that to my wife."

"He must wash my uniform first. There's no way I'm going to work like this. What will I say to the matron, huh, tell me?" asked the nurse.

"I just bought this jacket for R700. How will I get the stains out?" asked the woman sitting next to the nurse. "You must give me the money to buy stain remover."

By the time the taxi reached Bara Hospital I was sober again and I had a lot of washing to do for the passengers.

The taxi came to a standstill after the guy who had my vomit on his trousers had shouted "bus stop" after the BP Garage in Bara. Together with the nurse he stepped out of the taxi, but as he did so, he pulled me by my left leg.

I tried to wrench myself free, but his grip was too strong. I lost my balance and fell from my seat. As I fell, my leather jacket hooked itself on the metal edge of the seat and the inner part was torn out. A punch landed on the bridge of my nose and blood came out of my nose and mouth.

"Shaya!" shouted the nurse as she encouraged the guy to beat me.

"Ho! That's enough, we have to go now!" the taxi driver said as the taxi rolled forward. "That will teach you not to drink," he continued, smiling a wolfish, unsympathetic smile.

I kept quiet for the rest of my journey, but the other passengers called me every name they could lay their tongues on.

At the Green Church in Chi, by the robots, I got out of the taxi. The passengers were still laughing at me.

It was getting late, but I decided to take a shortcut that I knew. As I stopped to urinate at the side of the road, I saw a group of young guys, who were probably still in high school, sitting on the pavement just ahead of me. The guys started to act suspiciously as I passed them. They immediately stopped their conversation and whistled.

"Heita. Do you have a match?" one of the guys asked, approaching me with a cigarette between his lips.

The guy was wearing baggy jeans and an oversized T-shirt. He walked towards me, his thick chains shining on his chest, with the lumbering gait of tsotsis and gangster rappers.

"I don't smoke," I lied.

"Why do you walk alone at night without a match?"

I didn't answer him. I was panicking, anticipating all the nasty things that they were going to do to me.

As I looked back, to assess my chances of getting away, I heard an unfriendly voice behind me.

"Don't fuckin' move!" came the command and I heard the sound of a gun being cocked at the back of my head. "Don't look at us, just get down on your knees, bitch."

"Please, don't kill me!" I pleaded as I did as he commanded. "You can take anything you want, but please don't kill me."

"Who told you to speak?" asked one of the guys. "We'll decide what to do with you."

I kept quiet as I could see that pleading would only get me into trouble, but as I knelt in the street fear and hope gripped me simultaneously.

"Now, take everything out of your pockets, and I mean everything, including your cellphone and wallet, and put them on the ground."

Out of my pockets came my Ericsson cellphone, my wallet, which contained my cards and money, as well as the pieces of cheese, samoosas and chicken wings that I had taken from the party.

I heard the guys laughing and one of them picked up one of the chicken wings and started to eat it.

"Now, put your bag down, take off your leather jacket and your watch and put them on the ground."

"Yes, and take off your shoes too," added the guy that was eating the chicken wing. "Very nice suede, huh?"

"And those jeans too," added the third guy.

One of the guys jerked me up as if I weighed nothing.

"They're Diesel. Take them off as well."

"Leave him the T-shirt, it's a no-name piece of shit," the guy with the gun in his hand said.

One of the guys pinned me down against the tarmac and instructed me to make love to it. My teeth began to chatter.

"Now, I think you still want to live," said the guy who in the meantime had finished the chicken wing and started on a piece of cheese. "So, what's your PIN for this card?"

"I don't work and there's no money in the account. I'm a student and I just arrived from Cape Town," I responded nervously.

"Hey, don't insult my intelligence," he said in a threatening tone of voice. He raised his hand, but the klap I was expecting never came.

"My pin is 9797," I lied, my teeth still chattering as if it were a cold day.

"You're lying!"

"I'm not lying, I'm a student," I said, afraid that he would send his cronies to the nearest ATM to check if the number I had given him worked, but, to my immense relief, his tone suddenly changed.

"Oh, so you're a UCT student?" he said, holding up my student card. "And Mama and Papa are rich." His tone was heavy with sarcasm as he flashed the R480 that he had just taken from my wallet. "Chizboy, bhujwa, snob, huh?"

I could feel their eyes on me in the dim light.

"Where do you stay?" he asked.

"Here in Chi, at Midway."

"What sport did you do at varsity? Did you do sprinting?"

"Yes."

"Say 'Yes, sir!'" he commanded.

"Yes, sir."

"Now, hold your rusty keys in your right hand and this old bag in your left. When you hear the sound of the gun, you must run hard and never look back. Do you hear me?"

I nodded.

"Say 'Yes, sir!'"

"Yes, sir."

146

"Okay, on your marks!"

I put one knee down on the hard tarmac, preparing to run for my life.

"Ready? Go!"

As soon as I heard the gunshot ring out, I ran like a headless chicken. I was naked apart from my socks, my black boxers and my T-shirt. Luckily, my degree certificate and my statement of results were still in my old bag.

TWENTY
Friday, January 14

A headache was hammering away inside my head when I woke up on Friday morning. As I boiled water in my uncle's blackened pot on the double hotplate, the harsh reality of my swollen lips and sore ribs made me face facts: I had no cellphone, no watch and no money. Luckily, the thugs hadn't taken my fake degree certificate and statement of results.

As soon as I had finished my bath and dressed, Mama and Yuri arrived with sis Zinhle in her white VW Golf.

"I tried to call you last night and your phone rang just once and then you switched it off. I wanted to tell you that we'll be going to the hospital to visit your uncle early this morning. Lots of people are coming, including your sister, Nina. She's probably on her way as we speak," said Mama.

"Sorry about that, Mama, but I no longer have a phone."

"What happened to the one you had?"

"I was robbed by some thugs there by the Green Church when I came back last night."

"What?"

Mama came closer and examined my swollen lip. She put her comforting hand on my shoulder, but I ignored it.

"Are you okay, my baby? Did they injure you?" she asked.

"I'm fine, Mama."

"You did well to give them your cellphone," said sis Zinhle. "Nowadays these thugs will kill you for that toy."

"You must come and live with us in Naturena, Bafana. It's safe in the suburbs," said Mama, looking at me with a mixture of pity and concern. "Look at you, you're losing weight. This is not your body! You're not eating properly. You must come to Naturena so that I can cook for you."

"I will, Mama."

"And remind me, after the hospital, to go and buy a new cellphone for you."

"What will happen to Zero? Are the new owners going to let him stay in his zozo?" I asked, trying to steer the conversation away from myself.

"I don't know," Mama said. "He'll have to negotiate with them."

Nina arrived fifteen minutes later. By then I was recounting my ordeal for a second time to PP, Dilika and Zero, who had arrived in Zero's taxi.

As soon as everyone had arrived we all climbed into Zero's taxi. Zero drove it down to the corner of our street. A small group of women were standing there, as it was fah-fee time again, and I suddenly realised how much I missed my uncle.

Zero blew the taxi's horn and Priest Mthembu appeared wearing his favourite navy suit, a waistcoat and a paisley tie. He joined sis Zinhle on the middle seat where she was busy twisting Yuri's hair into small dreadlocks. Meanwhile, Nina was busy whispering gossip into my ear about sis Dudu. She told me that sis Dudu had agreed to visit my uncle, but had declined to come with us in Zero's taxi. She hated PP with such a passion that she had preferred to use her own transport.

At the robots by the Regina Mundi Catholic church we saw a

large crowd of people. Zero hooted for the people to clear the way and then slowed down. Although the robots were green, it was difficult to pass because of all the people in the road. We spotted a naked man sitting on the pavement; his hands had been handcuffed around the pole of the robot and a cardboard sign had been draped around his neck. Nina laughed out loud and pointed at the man with her manicured finger.

"Look at the sign, Bafana," she said.

We all looked at the sign. On it was written:

don't worry about me
I don't need your stupid help because I'm a thief

Zero hooted again as two potential passengers tried to flag our taxi down. We didn't stop, but it was easy to tell that Zero would have loved to have picked them up by the way he looked at them.

"People here in Folks Lake are cruel," said uBaba Mfundisi as Zero put on a pair of mirrored shades to prevent the sun from blinding him as he was driving.

"That man has been handcuffed to that pole since six this morning when I did my first load," said Zero as he drove slowly away from the crowd.

"I don't think he's from here in Folks Lake. Someone would have helped him a long time ago if he was from around here. He was probably dumped here," reasoned sis Zinhle.

I was still struggling to erase the image of the thief when Zero turned into the entrance at Bara Hospital. After signing the register, Zero drove us to a multistorey building with a big billboard on the front of it advertising a cellphone company.

By the time we had found our way to Block C, sis Dudu and her daughter, Palesa, were already there. The silence inside the ward and the face of the nurse standing next to sis Dudu were answer enough to our questions.

We circled my uncle's bed. His face was expressionless. There wasn't anything in his big dark eyes to signal that he was still alive.

"What happened to his hands?" asked sis Zinhle, touching my uncle's hands.

"He's in a vegetative state," the nurse said, "but he's also suffering from epileptic fits."

Sis Dudu's eyes grew watery and Mama drew in a little breath. I watched sis Dudu's unabashed tears flowing down her cheeks. Although she and my uncle hadn't been on speaking terms for about six years, she obviously felt pity for him. Like everyone else, she was shocked at what she had just heard, but I think seeing PP also had an effect on her as she began to sob uncontrollably. Seeing him there seemed to have opened up the unforgettable wounds of the past. Eventually, Priest Mthembu took her outside.

It had all started back in Chi, when sis Dudu had laid a charge against PP for attempted rape. Uncle Nyawana was against it and sis Dudu believed that he had accepted a bribe from PP to discourage her from going to the police. In time, the docket she opened at Protea North Police Station also got lost, which resulted in the case being dropped. I guess seeing PP reminded her of her agony.

She had been alone in our house in Chi. Palesa, who was very young at the time, was playing diketo on the street with the other kids. Nina and I were at school and both my uncles, Nyawana and Guava, were out. Mama and Aunt Thandi were also out at work. I had been told that PP had come into our house when sis Dudu was busy taking a bath in the bedroom. Sis Dudu hadn't suspected anything as there was music playing on the radio.

PP locked both doors to the house with the keys that we always left on the rack. After he had done that, he turned up the volume on the radio. By the time sis Dudu suspected something, PP was already outside the bedroom where she was busy taking her bath in a plastic basin. Seeing him come through the door, sis Dudu screamed and quickly put a towel around her waist. PP closed the door behind him and, within a minute, they were wrestling for the towel. Luckily for sis Dudu, Uncle Guava came home and heard her screaming.

"What are you doing in there? Open the goddamn door!" he shouted. "Why have you locked the door during the day?"

Sis Dudu screamed harder and Uncle Guava followed the noise and peeped through the window, which was slightly open. As he reached in and from outside drew the curtain back, he saw her sitting on the mat in the bedroom and crying, but by that time PP was nowhere to be seen. Reluctantly, sis Dudu went to the kitchen door to open it for Uncle Guava. She narrated her story to him and, after she had finished, they went to the police station to lay a charge. Uncle Guava was a witness, as he had seen PP's car parked outside on the pavement when he arrived home, but was surprised to find that PP had gone by the time he persuaded sis Dudu to open the door.

When they came back home from the police station, Uncle Nyawana was home and he looked drunk. He accused sis Dudu of being a liar. When he asked her to go and retract her statement, she refused. That's when she left him. Twenty days later the police had still not submitted the case to the prosecutors. Later they told sis Dudu that the docket had been lost.

Back in the ward I watched the tears gathering in Mama's eyes.

"My son," she said, grabbing my hand possessively. "I want you to pack your things and leave that ghost house. Enough is enough! I want you to come and live with us in Naturena. You can't live there alone! Both my parents died there, my sister died there, my brother was taken to jail from that house and the other one is about to die because of it." She caught her breath. "No, it's enough now! We must live!"

TWENTY-ONE
Monday, January 24

On Monday, a week after we had all gone to see my uncle in hospital, I secured a place to run my office from at the Mangalani BP Garage complex in Chi. It was a large room that had been a hair salon up until recently. Yomi was to operate his new internet café next door in another large room that had been a spaza shop. There was a door that linked the two rooms and we decided that we'd leave it unlocked, so that we could both have free access to both rooms. The acrid smell of the new paint filled the air, but it didn't bother me at all, I was too excited about opening my office.

I had withdrawn R4 000 from the R18 000 that was left in my bank account. We were supposed to be paying rent of R3 000 a month, excluding water and electricity, but we had agreed to share those expenses equally. However, we were also required to pay a deposit, and that was why we had to pay R3 000 each for the first month.

Vee came by in the afternoon to help me clean and decorate the place. I was expecting Yomi to come with furniture and computers the following day.

"Do you trust Yomi?" asked Vee as she hung my framed degree certificate on the wall.

"I don't know . . ." Our eyes met briefly. "But he seems like a guy with a lot of clever business ideas to me. What do you think?"

"All I can say is that you should pick your friends with great care," she warned.

"Why?"

She looked at my certificate for a second, but said nothing.

"I don't know, Bee," she said, shifting her eyes to the small book-shelf where I had put my collection of law books. "It's just that I've heard stories about him."

"What stories?" I asked.

"Are you aware that he also doubles as a pastor?"

"What? He never told me anything about that."

"Oh yes, he's a pastor at the International Christian Pentecostal Mission Church. The headquarters of his church are in Nigeria. My friend told me that people in the church are involved in drug traf-ficking."

"Is that so? I didn't know that."

"Yeah, well, I don't know about that, but I do know that people flock to his church because they think he possesses healing pow-ers."

"Maybe it's true," I said.

"You know what I've heard?" she began hesitantly, her eyes never leaving my face. "I've heard that he comes to church with people who pretend to be cripples in wheelchairs. During his sermon he puts his hands on them and pretends to be praying for them. He asks the cripples to rise up and walk in the name of the Lord, just like Jesus did in the Bible, and at the end of the sermon the cripples pretend to be normal again. That's why he's so popular in Yeoville." She paused. "He must like you a lot to trust you as his business partner . . ."

My conversation with Vee was disturbed by loud singing coming from outside. A group of people were toyi-toying along the Old Potchefstroom Road. They were heading for the Stars Soccer Fields. Five minutes later I heard a loud knock at the door. It was Zero.

"The revolution will not be televised, Advo. Do you realise that there's no water or electricity in most of Chi, including at our house?" said Zero.

"What?" I said, pinching the bridge of my nose.

I recalled that the switches were dead when I had come back from Naturena that morning. At the time I had thought it was due to the usual problem with the old power station in Orlando East.

"Siriyasi, Advo, these capitalists have removed the cables. Ever since we voted for them they don't give a fuck about us any more," said Zero, anger registering in his face. "They claim that we are stealing their electricity. To get reconnected we need to pay one thousand five hundred bucks. That's why there's an urgent meeting today. The residents are angry, Advo. I've never seen people as angry with the government."

"Where's the meeting?"

"At the Stars Soccer Fields. We have to go there right now. The revolution will not be televised, kuzonyiwa vandag. I-government isijwayela amasimba! The government is taking us for shit! This is Msawawa, our matchbox city, and we'll show them like we showed the apartheid government before them."

I looked at Vee. "I won't be long," I said.

"No, take your time. I'll have time to decide where to put these pictures," she said, as I walked out of the office with Zero.

* * *

ANTI-PRIVATISATION FORUM (APF)

SOWETO ELECTRICITY CRISIS COMMITTEE

HIV/Aids + PREPAID = 100% DEATH RATE

declared the three red banners that had been hung from the cross-bar of a goal at one end of the Stars Soccer Fields. Approximately five hundred people had already gathered and there were also six or seven police vans. Zero and I mingled with the angry crowd. A woman was busy talking on a loudspeaker; she was standing on an oil drum that had been converted into a makeshift stage and placed on the penalty spot.

"We say away with the installation of prepaid meters, away!" shouted the woman, her fist raised in the air.

"Away!" responded the crowd, their fists also raised in the air.

"We say that six thousand litres of free water from the government is not enough. My own family consumes that ration in just five days, comrades, because there are twenty-two of us living in one house. I'm unemployed. How does the government think I will pay for water for the remainder of the month?" continued the woman.

"You're right, comrade!" we shouted.

"We say down with the installation of prepaid electricity, down!"

"Down!" we responded.

"Water is life, comrades! We used to pay cheaper flat rates for water and electricity during apartheid. Why do we have to have this expensive prepaid with a black ANC government? Why are we, the poor people, discriminated against by our own government?"

"Viva, comrade!"

"We must boycott the local government elections, comrades, be-cause it's clear now that when we voted them into power for the

157

second time their campaign was based on a set of false promises. They are only interested in exchanging the riches of this country with white people."

"Yes, comrade," the people shouted.

"These politicians talk like angels when they need our votes, but behave like chimpanzees once they've got them. We can't sit back and watch them destroy our lives by removing our water and electricity. In the past we've fought and defeated the monster of apartheid, comrades. Amandla, comrades, amandla!"

"Amandla!"

"Now, we're faced with the monster of capitalism here in the township. It's time for this government to deliver on their promises! Their honeymoon is over! Prepaid is illegal in the UK, Uruguay and the Netherlands, comrades! Why not here in Mzansi?"

"Viva, comrade, viva!"

"We must fight the monster of capitalism, not next year, not next month, not next week, but today, comrades! Where does this government think we'll get the money to pay for their services? We need jobs and not the prepaid water and electricity meters. Away with the meters, away!"

"Away!"

"It's this prepaid water that led to the outbreak of cholera in Kwa-Zulu, comrades, because our people can't afford to buy the water. Our brothers and sisters are dying there and all the government is doing is showing them the finger." The lady raised her fat middle finger.

Most of the comrades laughed.

"We say prepaid water and electricity is unconstitutional!"

158

"Viva, comrade, viva!" the crowd responded.

"We must go house by house, starting here in Chi, and pull out the newly installed meters. We have fifteen comrades among us who are retrenched electricians and plumbers. For safety reasons, they are the ones that will pull out the meters. We urge comrades from all affected areas – Mogale City, Nelspruit, Kagiso and Stutterheim – to do the same."

Somebody started a political song as the leader of the crowd climbed down from the oil drum.

Mshin'wam, mshin'wam. (My machine gun, my machine gun.)
Awuleth'umshin'wam. (Bring me my machine gun.)

Singing and clapping their hands, the crowd followed the woman as she turned into the street that led towards the Old Potchefstroom Road. The police vans followed them with sirens blaring.

I dodged Zero, and the crowd, and walked in the opposite direction towards my new office. As I passed the parking lot, next to the Absa bank, I saw sis Zinhle's VW Golf and realised that I had visitors.

As I entered the office I saw that Mama and Priest Mthembu were there as well. Sis Zinhle was staring at my degree certificate on the wall, making me feel deeply uncomfortable.

"Mmmmmm! Your office looks beautiful, congratulations!" said sis Zinhle.

"Thanks."

"We've come from visiting your uncle in hospital," said Mama, also staring at the certificate as if she saw a new kind of Kuzwayo dignity in it, "but I thought I should pass by to give you the new cellphone that I bought for you. And uBaba Mfundisi also wanted to see your new workplace and bless it with a prayer."

"Sawubona, Baba Mfundisi," I greeted Priest Mthembu as I shook his hand.

"Sawubona, mfanawam."

"How is my uncle doing?" I asked Mama.

"At least the doctors say that there is improvement this time," explained Mama.

There was a moment of silence as Priest Mthembu examined my certificate with great admiration.

"This is a good thing for the people of this township," he said, smiling expansively. "I think God has answered our prayers. We must thank Him with a prayer. Let's all close our eyes and ask for His blessings."

I didn't close my eyes as Priest Mthembu began his prayer, but the rest of them did.

"Lord, help our children to know the road that You've chosen for them. Sustain them with Your strength and let them not be satisfied with selfish goals. Help us, Father, to take our talents and to lay them on the altar of Your service, that we too may be used to bring others to You. Help us to live so that by the wisdom of our words and the power of our example many more may be moved to give their minds and hearts to You. God, our Father, hear this prayer. Amen!"

Priest Mthembu excused himself after saying the prayer, but Mama, sis Zinhle and Vee stayed to watch me put the sign on the door. The sign read:

B. KUZWAYO

ATTORNEYS

TEL: 011 984 3610

On the door to Yomi's shop I put another sign that read:

INTERNET SERVICE = R5/HOUR

PHOTOCOPY = 50C/PAGE

PRINTING = R2/PAGE

FAX (LOCAL) = R3/PAGE

All the time Mama was looking at me. Her eyes were bright with pride, but I just felt like a criminal. My heart was thumping hard. I hoped that no one asked me why I had put "attorneys" instead of "advocates" on my sign.

"What was the toyi-toying all about anyway?" asked Mama.

"Well, people are protesting against the installation of prepaid water and electricity," I said.

"Why?" sis Zinhle asked with disbelief. "I mean, the government has promised to write off all their debts if the people agree on the installation. Isn't that a good thing, chomza, huh?" She looked at Mama for reassurance. "You said that you owe about R14 000 in unpaid services. Imagine what that could do for someone experiencing financial problems, chomza?"

"But, chomza, most people are unemployed here in the township. How does the government think we'll pay for the services? Imagine pensioners being expected to pay for these services and buy food with the peanuts that the government is handing out to them from its pension fund. It's really unfair!" reasoned Mama.

"But nothing is for free in this world, chomza, and the people must learn. I heard that the government is willing to give six kilolitres of water and fifty kilowatts of electricity per month to those who allow the prepaid water and electricity meters to be installed. Is that not generous?" asked sis Zinhle.

"Yes, but we voted for this government because they promised to improve our lives," said Mama.

"They've already done that. Look! They've built roads. It's easy to drive on the Old Potchefstroom Road because it's four lanes now instead of only two. People don't have to pay to go to the clinics. Tokoza Park is well maintained. Unemployed people with children younger than fourteen get welfare grants. I just don't know what more people want."

"But, sis Zinhle, that's just a cosmetic change," I said. "We really appreciate those changes, but there is a lot that is still to be done. I mean, many people are still homeless and need better houses and jobs. These meters simply mean that before we have water and electricity we must have cash. You can only have money if there is a job for you. Otherwise people will resort to crime."

I don't think sis Zinhle accepted my point of view, but there was no further comment from her. I think she was just afraid of challenging a qualified advocate.

"Anyway, we're here to give you your new cellphone and to see your new office," said Mama, handing me a new Nokia 6110. "You're coming to Naturena this weekend, aren't you, baby?"

"Oh, yes, I'll be there."

"Why don't you bring Vee along so that she can see my place," she said, looking at Vee, who returned her smile.

TWENTY-TWO
Monday, January 31

A week had passed since I had opened my office in Chi, but my headache was still how to find clients. The internet café was making money as the unemployed youth from Chi and neighbouring Mapetla and Protea used it to apply for jobs and type their CVs, but the internet café wasn't part of my business, it was Yomi's. It was month-end and I had to pay my share of the rent: R1 500, plus water and electricity.

Besides the rent, my other concern was my image and I had decided to use part of the R14 000 that was left in my bank account to buy proper clothes. Mama had raised a further R2 000 for me, which she wanted me to spend on some formal clothes for myself, including a gown which I could wear to court.

At nine that morning I was already in Zero's taxi on my way to the city to buy a gown and a suit at Markhams. In my pocket I had R4 000: R2 000 from Mama and R2 000 that I had withdrawn from Absa. The taxi was already full and Zero took a different route from his usual one as he tried to avoid the Old Potchefstroom Road that, he complained, was full of robots and traffic officers. In Dlamini, the taxi turned to the right between Ibhongo High School and the only mosque in Soweto.

"How is the business going, Advo? I see lots of people coming in and out of your pozi," Zero began.

"Not so bad, but at the moment I spend a lot of time at the Protea Magistrate's Court," I lied.

"I'll bring you more clients," he said with great authority in his voice. "The first one will be my Bunju. I've told you, she needs you to help her apply for a child grant for her son. She also wants advice on how she can make the father of her child pay maintenance."

"But she can go to the Welfare Department instead of coming to me," I said.

"Oh, I see," Zero said. "I'll tell her later."

There was silence between us as I helped him count the money that I had just collected from the passengers. As the taxi passed Reed Lake, which separates Dlamini and Kliptown, I gave Zero the R65 that I had collected.

"This place," said Zero as we passed the golf course in Pimville, "at this place I used to forage for paper, plastic and aluminium at Goudkoppies and sell it to waste recycling companies here in Kliptown. That's when I was staying in Pimville Zone 4. You know Goudkoppies, don't you, Advo?" he asked.

"No, I don't know it," I said, shaking my head.

Zero pointed at a heap of waste at the side of the road that separated Eldorado Park from Pimville. I saw two green-and-white Pikitup trucks dumping waste while people stood by and watched.

"Every day, I used to compete with about a thousand other people scavenging for paper and plastic, Advo. Just like those people you can see over there. I worked at Goudkoppies seven days a week for almost eight years, but I only ever made about R100 or R200 a week. I used to have sugared water and bread every day."

I was shocked into silence by the revelation.

"I think I know what poverty is, Advo. I used to dodge medical waste – used syringes, drips, bloody sheets and bandages – at the dump. I used to inhale toxic fumes from the degrading chemicals. We competed with well-fed scavenging rats this big." He demonstrated the size of the rat on the dashboard. "Those rats roamed the place so fearlessly. They would just stand there and continue eating as if we weren't there."

We passed Freedom Park squatter camp where the smell of sewage was very bad; it was as if someone with rotten bowels had farted inside the taxi. Most of the passengers closed their windows. As soon as we had come to a stop by the robots at the N1 off-ramp in Devland, Zero lifted his fingers up for me to see. There was a big scar across three of his fingers.

"This happened one day when I was digging through the garbage at Goudkoppies. The broken glass cut me. It was a very big gash. I thought it would never heal."

* * *

I arrived in the city at about twenty minutes to ten. I went straight to Markhams where I bought a black gown for R800. In the same shop I bought myself two suits, one black and the other navy, two ties and two pairs of shoes.

While I was still in the fitting rooms Yomi called to say that he was at our offices in Chi with the business cards he had printed for us. I asked him to wait there for me as I was almost done with my shopping.

It took me about half an hour to get a taxi back to Soweto as this time I didn't use Zero's taxi. As soon as I arrived at the Mangalani BP Garage I went straight to my office. Yomi was still there and the first thing that he let me see was my business card. It contained everything about my business, including a fake company registration number.

"That certificate looks real up there, my brother," he said, his face shining with satisfaction.

"Do you think so?" I asked nervously.

"Don't worry, my brother, no one is going to know, but you know what? I was having this conversation with my friend Tolu and he was suggesting that you need another certificate from the Board of Exam just to show that you were admitted as an attorney. You won't be able to appear in court without it."

"I know, but where am I going to get that?"

"My brother, there are lots of things that we can do together as long as you can pay."

"Can you really arrange that as well?"

"Yes, man, I can. I was thinking about Sunday. Are you free then?"

"Sounds like a plan."

"Good. Make some cash available."

"How much?"

"Make it a thousand."

"That's expensive, man."

Yomi's face took on a serious look, as if to warn me.

"My brother, life is full of promises that only money can answer. But, because it's you, I'll tell him to cut the price down by two hundred. You can make it eight hundred."

"Fine, it's a deal."

"Listen, my brother, I'm not staying today. I was only here to deliver two more computers and connect them. Now my job is done, so I'm leaving. Here are the rest of the business cards."

Yomi and I left about thirty minutes later. I went to Naturena as I wanted to show Mama the new clothes that I had bought, but when I reached Mama's place, at about five that afternoon, she was sitting on the sofa with her eyes bloodshot from weeping. The house was full of sadness. Even the television, which Yuri and Uncle Thulani's two kids were watching, was muted.

"The hospital just called. They say your uncle is on life-support," she said, giving a tearful protest as I sat down on the sofa.

TWENTY-THREE
Tuesday, February 1

I was sleeping in Naturena when I was woken by a call from a sergeant Nkuna from the Protea Magistrate's Court. It was half past
one in the morning. He told me that somebody by the name of Lifa
Makhanya had been arrested for assaulting another man in a shebeen and had named me as his lawyer. It was only when I spoke
to Lifa Makhanya on the phone that I realised it was Zero.

"Zero, what happened?" I asked.

"It was self-defence, Advo. Come and get me out. I can't sleep in
this place."

"But I'm in Naturena and I don't have a car, you know that."

"Ask bra Thulani or Zinhle, please, Advo."

"You know what time it is now, man? They're asleep. First thing
in the morning I'll be there."

I didn't sleep for the rest of the night. I was thinking about the
challenge that Zero's situation posed me. He had done me a lot of
favours, giving me all those free rides to the city, and I felt obliged
to pay him back.

Early that morning, I was on my way to Protea Magistrate's Court,
where Zero had been held overnight, carrying my bogus results under my arm in an envelope. When I had told Mama what had happened to Zero, she had given me the moral support that I needed
on what was going to be my first day in court.

"Come on, you can do it, Bafana," she had said.

Even dressed smartly in my new black suit, a pink tie and white

168

shirt, I found myself uttering Mama's exact words loudly to myself as I entered the gates of the Protea Magistrate's Court.

As soon as I arrived I had a brief talk with Sergeant Nkuna, who told me that Zero had insisted that he wanted to talk to me and no one else. Sergeant Nkuna took me down to see Zero and, to my surprise, I found that I knew the police guard at the cell door as he also lived in Chi. Inside the holding cell there were about eight more people that were all desperate for legal representation.

"It's always like that. Drink and driving, fights, rapes and killings, murder, robbery, housebreaking, you name it," said Sergeant Nkuna. "And they all claim they're innocent."

"Hectic," I said.

"You must give me your details because there are always people needing representation here. I can recommend you and the two of us can work well together, you know what I mean?"

I gave Sergeant Nkuna my card.

"Is this your first time representing someone here?" he asked, admiring my freshly printed business card.

"Yes."

"You know the procedure, don't you? You must go to the magistrate that's holding your case after talking to your client. Your case will be in Court 2D and the magistrate's name is Your Worship Moloi. You must go to his office, which is behind the court, and introduce yourself."

That was helpful information, but since I'd come back to Soweto from Cape Town I'd been observing how things were done. Even in Cape Town I'd often attended Wynberg Magistrate's Court. There, in particular, I had learned a lot of things. I was even there when two bogus lawyers were busted while busy making an application for bail on behalf of their client. They made the mistake of calling a magistrate Your Majesty instead of Your Worship.

Sergeant Nkuna left me alone with Zero. His right eye was swollen and blackened.

"What happened?" I asked Zero as we sat down and talked in the room just outside the cell.

"I was drinking at the Out Of Control Tavern with Bunju at about eleven last night when her ex-boyfriend came in with his friend. He was drunk and he wanted to take her away from me, but she refused to go with him. He hit her, and when I tried to protect her, he drew a knife on me and threatened to butcher me. As he did that I blocked the knife and cracked my bottle of Hansa on his skull. His friends attacked me, but the owner of the tavern called the police. When they arrived I was arrested immediately. You should have seen the blood, Advo. I'm not proud of what I did to him, but it was in self-defence. He would have killed me. I had to call you. I don't have enough zak for other lawyers, but you can represent me on credit, as a friend. I'll get some zak soon. I just don't want to spend another night in here."

"It's not about money, bra Zero," I said. "It's about the court experience that I don't have. You should have called one of the legal aid attorneys. They would have represented you for free."

"I don't trust babuelli basechaba," he said in Sesotho. "They're always unprepared, Advo. Besides, you know me better than them. We're friends, and I trust you, you see."

"What's the name of the officer that arrested you?"

"Sergeant Ngobese."

I left Zero in the holding cell and went to the office of magistrate Moloi. It was about half past nine when I knocked at the open office door and the robeless magistrate Moloi invited me in with a wave of his hand.

"Young man, what can I do for you?" he said, busy writing something in a file.

"My name is Bafana Kuzwayo and I'll be the one representing Mr Lifa Makhanya who is appearing in Your Worship's court at eleven this morning. He was arrested yesterday by Sergeant Ngobese for assault," I said quickly, my knees and ankles quivering with every step that I made across the floor of his office.

"Is it your first time in this court, Mr Kuzwayo?" he asked as if I had said something wrong.

"Yes, Your Worship."

I was expecting him to ask me about my certificates, but to my relief he just looked at me once and then looked back at his diary. He was obviously too busy to verify my credentials, but panic was causing my heart to hit my chest hard.

"Listen, Mr Kuzwayo, I have about eight hundred defendants under indictment, let's talk about this case fast."

"Certainly, Your Worship."

He looked at me for a while, his forehead creasing in concentration. The creases were arranged in such a way that I began to count them.

"Well, I assume that you're going to plead not guilty?"

"That's correct, Your Worship," I answered without thinking.

"Am I also correct in saying that you'll apply for bail on behalf of your client?"

"Yes, Your Worship."

"And why do you think that I should grant your client bail?"

"Because my client has never been convicted before, Your Worship. He has three kids that he's supporting and I'm afraid he might lose his job if he sleeps another night in the cells. He's not a danger to society and I don't think there's a risk that he might run away."

"Where does your client work?"

"He's a taxi driver, Your Worship."

"Well, I'll grant bail as is routine for a first court appearance. I will make the whole thing very quick. It won't last for more than five minutes. Do you understand?" he said, glancing at his watch.

His words delighted me.

"Have you met Mr Khoza, the prosecutor in this case?" he asked.

"Not yet, Your Worship, but I thought I'd meet him immediately after talking to you."

I had been told by Sergeant Nkuna that I would already find the prosecutor in Court 2D as he always arrived about an hour early. As I entered Court 2D, I saw a man with a shaved head sitting on the bench opposite that of the magistrate. He fitted Sergeant Nkuna's description of Mr Khoza, but he was also a guy I was familiar with, although I had never known his name or talked to him before. I went and introduced myself.

* * *

At eleven o'clock Bunju, PP, Dilika, Nina and her boyfriend, Bheki, sis Zinhle, Mama and Uncle Thulani were all in the courtroom as Zero emerged from the holding cells. There were about thirty people in the courtroom. We all rose to our feet as the magistrate sneaked in from the back door. Mama winked at me and I winked back as the magistrate gave a quick synopsis of the case that didn't even last five minutes.

I watched Zero leap into the air with excitement as the magistrate announced that he was going to be released on bail. Within seconds, I was covered by the perfumed bodies of Nina, Bunju, Mama and sis Zinhle, while my hand was shaken many times as Dilika and PP congratulated me on my first successful case.

PP paid Zero's bail of R600, and the case was set for the 26th of February, but the gossip about me winning cases had already raced back to Chi. It was rumoured that Zero would have got more than ten years in prison if it had not been for my brilliance and that the magistrate was no match for me. Mama was the proudest mother in the whole of the township.

TWENTY-FOUR
Monday, February 14

Although the sale of the house in Chi had still not gone through, I was spending more of my time in Naturena. I had met a girl called Lerato and she lived quite close to Mama's place. My business still wasn't doing very well in terms of making money. Most of the clients I represented were poor and paid me in small instalments, but I still had R9 000 left in my bank account from the money Mama had given me.

I started to prepare for my Valentine's Day date with Lerato at around eleven that morning. We had met a few weeks earlier at Southgate Mall when we had found ourselves sitting next to each other in the taxi back to Naturena. Already we had planned a very romantic day over the phone and she had agreed to come to Mama and Uncle Thulani's house. Our plan was to go to Zoo Lake near Rosebank Mall as there was a music festival going on there. To welcome my Lerato I had bought a large slab of chocolate that I had got nicely wrapped at a nearby gift shop.

Unfortunately, Lerato's first visit to Mama's place turned out to be a total disaster. Mama did not approve of my relationship with her and she had made it quite clear to me that she preferred Vee. According to Mama, Lerato was a snob. She hated the fact that Lerato spoke English with a nasal private-school accent as if she had no chest.

"As a respected lawyer, Bafana," Mama said to me the day I introduced her to Lerato, "you're supposed to be seen with someone with good manners, like Vee. That private-school child undermines our African way of life; I haven't once heard her speak Sesotho."

"But you've just met her, Mama, how can you judge her? Besides, even the so-called black intelligentsia speak English amongst themselves."

"English, my balls! Who's going to preserve our culture if we don't speak our own language?"

"But the only black people that are preserving their culture are those that find it difficult to rise above the yoke of poverty, Mama. They're the ones selling fruit and vegetables in spaza shops and chicken feet on the pavements."

"But how does that link to speaking African languages?"

"You can't think big in African languages, Mama, and you can't move out of the township either. I don't want to be trapped in Soweto forever. You know, when I enter our family house in Chi I can smell the poverty inside."

"Did they teach you this shit in your university?" she asked, clicking her tongue in disgust.

It was about one thirty in the afternoon when Lerato knocked at the door. I was in my room, but through the lace curtains I saw her coming confidently up the driveway. She was dressed in a blue cap, a white denim miniskirt and a red top that framed her curves articulately.

Lerato knocked just once at the door and then, without waiting for anyone to answer, she opened it, entered, and pushed it shut again. As she did that I could imagine Mama's eyeballs growing hot with anger. She was watching TV with Uncle Thulani, Yuri and Uncle Thulani's two kids from his previous marriage.

I heard Mama clicking her tongue as she muted the TV, but Lerato ignored the warning and, while I watched stealthily from behind my door, she continued to wind Mama up.

"Where's Bamfan?" she asked, her nasal pronunciation of my name making Mama grimace in disgust.

"Good afternoon to you too," Mama said sarcastically, trying to sound like her. "This is not Bamfan's house. You must learn to greet the people you find inside when entering other people's houses," she continued in a dismissive manner, "and you must remove your cap when entering my house in future."

"Well, I'm sah-ree," Lerato said, removing her blue cap. "Is Bamfan in?"

"Okay, Lee-rat-oh," Mama said slowly, mimicking her accent. "Did he tell you that this was his house? Because we have rules in here."

"I didn't come here to see you. I've come to see Bamfan," Lerato insisted.

"Your Bamfan did not just drop from the sky, you know, Lee-rat-oh. He's my son and I gave birth to him," said Mama as the two of them stared at one another with hatred.

"I know that. It's obvious because you're pregnant even now."

"Fine, if that's how your parents raised you, but I won't tolerate your bad manners in this house. I think you should leave."

"Okay, fine, I'm leaving your house now."

Mama stood up and slammed the door violently behind her as I came out of my room. She stared at me intently, as if I had just brought an evil spirit into her house. I believe if she had looked into the mirror at that moment, it would have cracked. I looked away.

"Oh, that girl! I don't want to see her in my house again! You must meet her in the street," she said, opening her eyes wide and peering at my anxious face. "Do you hear me, Bafana?"

"Yebo, Mama."

By the time I made it out of the house, Lerato was sniffling in the driveway. She wiped her nose noisily with the back of her hand and then opened the gate into the street. I followed her.

"Lerato! Please talk to me!" I pleaded.

She stood and glared at me for a moment and walked away.

"I can't talk to you while you still live with that arrogant mother of yours," she said, her tone of voice warning me that she was very angry.

"Let's talk about it," I insisted.

"What's there to talk about, huh? You heard her! I came in a good mood. We'd been planning this day, Bamfan, but your mom has spoiled it already. I'm not her daughter. This is the new millennium! Jeeeez! Even Granny wasn't as old-fashioned."

"But, look, it's her house and I'm . . ."

"Okay, fine, you can take her side if you want. I don't care any more. She's your mom and blood is thicker than water. Just stop following me, please!"

I didn't know what to say to appease her and when I tried to catch up with her, Lerato started to walk faster.

"Stop following me, please! I need some space to breathe!" she said, with a hint of anger in her eyes.

"Please, love, we can work this out."

She retreated into a shell of silence, but I kept following her. Then, out of the blue, a Barry White song came into my head.

"You know that you're my first, my last, my everything," I sang.

"I don't care! Just leave me alone!" she shouted without trimming her stride.

I breathed a sigh of frustration and, unwillingly, I gave up following her.

Instead of going back to the house to face another moral lecture from Mama, I went straight to the Jazz Syndrome pub. It was just a few streets from Mama's house and I had discovered it the very first week I had begun spending more time in Naturena.

Along the way I envied the young couples that I passed, as they strolled aimlessly hand in hand. I was sure that I couldn't continue to stay with Mama. I had slowly come to realise that Mama was very strict and I was sure that if I stayed much longer with her in Naturena, she would discover that I had failed my degree. I missed Uncle Nyawana and the freedom I had enjoyed at our house in Chi. He was still on life-support at the hospital and I had hoped to visit him with Vee over the weekend, but Vee was in Zimbabwe for a week to sort out some problems with her work permit. At least he had had time before his accident to teach me that alcohol and dagga were a wonderful way to transcend unhappiness.

* * *

At half past three that afternoon I was still sitting on a bar stool in the Jazz Syndrome pub. Apart from two couples dancing to Don Laka's "Mamelodi", the place was empty.

I ordered another packet of Craven A cigarettes and another double tot of J&B on the rocks. Although I was not a great fan of jazz, the music was easing my mind, allowing me to think clearly about my situation. I was trying to think of a way of convincing Mama to allow me to rent my own space in the township once the sale of the house finally went through.

Don Laka's song ended and some deep jazz that immediately irritated me started to play. It was not my kind of music. To me it sounded like I was in a dense jungle listening to the movement of snakes and spiders. It filled me with sorrow.

I knew the song was "Meditation Suite" by Bheki Mseleku. Sis Zinhle and Mama adored the song and every time it was played sis Zinhle would spread her arms wide, stomp her right foot on the floor like a small, over-excited girl and shout, "Uuuuuhhhhhh, umkhaya-wam wase Thekwini!"

Sis Zinhle would then go on to claim that her father, uBaba Sokhulu, came from the same area in Durban as Bheki Mseleku, and Mama would always respond by adding that Mseleku was South Africa's answer to John Coltrane. I didn't know who Coltrane was and I didn't care.

As I sat at the bar the instrument in the song that sounded like a guitar went "diiinng", as if a mosquito had just passed my ear. Then there was a pause in the song for about ten seconds before another instrument, that sounded like a bass guitar, went "dooonng", as if the mosquito were coming back to bite me.

After about an hour and a half some more people came into the pub. The majority of them were older than me. Not long after that, sis Zinhle herself walked in. She was wearing a red skirt with a belt and a white knitted top. She walked in slowly, as if the pub were holding a beauty contest and she was one of the beautiful girls that everyone had to watch and vote for. As soon as I realised that she was alone, I waved to her to come and sit next to me. I was desperate to talk to somebody. I thought that I could ask her how I could win my Lerato back.

"Thank you, Bafana," she said as I grabbed a bar stool and put it next to me, "but what is an advocate like you doing here?"

"Well, I got bored sitting at home alone."

Sis Zinhle gave me three rapid nods.

"I believe you," she said sarcastically. "Where is Vee?"

"She's still in Zim."

"Well, it's a good thing that you're here, otherwise I would be sitting all by myself in this bar staring at all these men," she said, making herself comfortable on the stool. "Or do you have some company?"

"No, I'm alone, although I'm inseparable from unhappiness."

"Why's that? Did Vee fire you?"

"No, it's Lerato. And, yes, I guess she fired me."

"Lerato? I don't know her. What did you do to her?"

"It's not me, it's Mama."

"What did chomza do to your girl now?"

"They had an argument."

"Pregnant women are always moody, you must know that. She'll be fine. I mean, your girlfriend."

"I hope so," I said with bewilderment. "And you? Why are you all alone on Valentine's Day?"

"Argh," she started in a disappointed tone. "I wish my husband, that idiot doctor, could hear you asking that question. He told me that he'd join me later. He said he was busy with some patients at his surgery."

180

"No way! He's working on Valentine's Day?"

"Sure, that's what he says, but I know he's lying. He's seeing a girl. I even know who she is. He's a complete arsehole," she said. "That's why I came here on my own. My cellphone is off," she declared, "and I have decided that I can enjoy life on my own."

At that moment she accidentally knocked her car keys that she had left on the bar to the ground. I noticed, for the first time, that sis Zinhle was already tipsy. I picked up her keys and put them back on the bar.

I had overheard Mama telling Uncle Thulani how sis Zinhle's husband had bought her the VW Golf that she drove after she had caught him screwing a woman in the back room of his surgery. Mama said that the car was a kind of apology.

"What would you like to drink?" I asked.

"I didn't know that you drank," she said, shooting me a puzzled glance.

Instead of responding to her, I said, "I'm having J&B on the rocks, but I know you prefer Amarula or cider when you're in the mood for drinking."

"Oh, that's what I want now," she replied, whacking her fist on the table. "I need something strong, and your uncle Nyawana's drink will do."

I ordered a J&B on the rocks for sis Zinhle, but as soon as it arrived she drained her glass without a pause and ordered another one.

"Mmmm, it tastes so good! I want another one, please! Why are you drinking so slowly, Advo?"

It was the first time she had ever called me that.

"The night is still young for me," I answered, twirling the ice in my drink.

I took out a cigarette, put it between my lips and lit a match, cupping the flame against an imaginary wind with my fingers.

"Can I taste that?" she asked as I lit my cigarette.

"Huh? But you don't smoke."

"Neither do you, so what's the fuss all about?"

While I lit another cigarette for her, the grin on her face suddenly collapsed.

"You can keep a secret, can't you, Advo?"

"Your secret is safe with me."

"It's actually a good thing that I found you here, but before I tell you anything, do you promise not to tell your mother or anyone else?"

"Yes, I promise. Trust me!"

"I want you to advise me on something personal since you're now a big lawyer in Chi. Consider what I'll tell you as the first major test in your bright career."

"Yes, I'm listening."

"I want to file for divorce and I'll pay you to advise me on the procedure."

"But I'm not an experienced lawyer yet," I confessed.

"I know that and that's why I want you to advise me on how I can do it – not to represent me in the court of law," she said.

I was relieved and decided to tell her what I had learned at law school about the irretrievable breakdown of marriage.

"Okay, on what grounds are you divorcing your husband?" I asked.

"I haven't had sex with that bastard for about six months now.

Every time he gives me the same excuse, that he's too tired. He no longer loves me because he's seeing someone else and he has a baby with her. You know, being loved is important because it facilitates the opportunity to love in return, Advo. Since she had the baby my husband changes his mind on things that are very important to our relationship like I change my hairstyle."

"I understand."

"You know, Advo, men surprise me. How can you plan with your partner for a week and then cancel at the last minute? How can he choose his patients over me? Is it because I'm no longer attractive?"

"No, you're very attractive," I stammered. "But, about the divorce thing, there are two places that I know of. The cheapest place is the Southern Divorce Courts. The other place is the High Court, which is a little expensive," I said, without much knowledge of what I was talking about.

"Money is not an issue, I want to divorce that man," she said, ordering another drink.

"Go file it with the High Court then."

Sis Zinhle wrinkled her nose and tried to smile.

"Ow! Your drink tastes nice. Do you take credit cards here?" she asked, looking up at the barman as he brought her another drink.

"Yes, mam," he replied.

A jazz song by Sipho Gumede started to play and most of the couples in the bar stood up and danced to it.

"Come and let me teach you my moves," said sis Zinhle, leading me to the dance floor.

I was reluctant, but her smile finally persuaded me. On the dance floor she turned and twisted seductively, pressing her body hard against mine. The heat that came from her body drove me wild. I was burning with the need for real closeness. Stealthily, I looked at her voluptuous cleavage and allowed a wave of desire to sweep over me. I licked my dry lips as I imagined her breasts inside her knitted top rubbing against my chest.

The song ended, and hand in hand we went back to the table and sipped what was left in our glasses. She had been magically transformed from the angry, depressed creature that I had been talking to earlier into the laughing woman that I knew as sis Zinhle.

"You know what, Advo, there's a very nice joint in Ridgeway called The Ridge. Would you like to go there with me?" she asked.

"Certainly."

"Can you drive?"

"Yes, but I'm afraid I'm too drunk tonight and, besides, I don't have a driver's licence."

"No stress," she replied, "I'll drive."

Inside the car, as sis Zinhle drove, her red skirt rode up to display her gorgeous thighs.

Fifteen minutes later we entered a small shopping complex next to Rifle Range Road. It was already midnight and the song "Wonderful Tonight" by Eric Clapton was busy serenading us from her CD player. She managed to park the car in the parking lot, but the two of us were enjoying the song so much that we stayed in the car for a little longer.

"If I had a girlfriend I would like her to look exactly like you," I said.

Sis Zinhle smiled. She didn't seem to notice that it was no longer Advo talking to her, but the whisky.

"Why?"

"Because you've got style. The way you dress. The way you talk. Just everything about you is wonderful!"

"Are you sure about what you're saying," she asked as if she were inhaling the words.

Very slowly, I touched her left thigh and within seconds our faces were moving closer together and my tongue slid deep into her mouth. We both smelled of cigarettes and booze, but that didn't prevent our tongues from snaking rhythmically to the song. Her driver's seat was transformed into a couch, and I pinned her down on her back.

"No, no, no," her voice was breathless and slurred, "this will keep your eager sperm away from my eggs."

She took a condom from her handbag in the glove compartment and handed it to me. I used my teeth to open it.

TWENTY-FIVE
Tuesday, February 15

At about half past nine in the morning the ringing of my cellphone forced me to wake up. My head was heavy from the night before, but Vee was already outside my office in Chi and she wanted us to talk seriously. She was back from Zimbabwe. Mama had gone to work and there were only Aunty Manto and Yuri in the house. Aunty Manto was busy washing clothes in the bathroom. I asked her to let me use the bathroom first as I was already late for work and she agreed.

I finished bathing and hurriedly dressed in my new navy suit that I had bought at Markhams a few weeks earlier. By ten o'clock I was in a taxi to Bara Taxi Rank where I had to catch another taxi to Chi. By the time I got to Chi, twenty minutes later, Vee was waiting for me at the fish-and-chips shop. She was reading a magazine and drinking a Coke.

I opened my office immediately and the two of us sat there facing each other.

"Bee," Vee said. "I want you to do me a favour."

"What kind of a favour?" I asked.

"Eh," she hesitated. "This is embarrassing, but I'm asking you because I'm in a desperate situation."

"Go on."

"You know that it's difficult to work in this country if you're not a South African?"

"I know. It's bad," I said.

186

"My problem is my work permit. I have a new one now, but I'm tired of going back home every three months to renew it."

My eyes were fixed on her lips as she was speaking. I noticed, for the first time, that her small, sharp nose spoilt whatever beauty her face had.

"So you want me to help you organise a longer work permit?"

"Actually, the favour that I want to ask you is a bit more than that. What I'm asking you will require you to suspend your respect for the law and your tradition." She paused. "I want you to marry me. I'll pay you fifteen grand."

"Marry you?" I asked in a shocked tone of a voice.

"Yes."

I scratched my head and looked away briefly in thought. Fifteen grand was a lot of money. I only had R8 000 of Mama's money left, and Vee's money would help me pay rent for the office.

"I know we're just friends," she said, looking away and then back at me, "but I'm desperate."

I thought for a while, but deep in my heart I knew that I needed the cash.

"I want to help you, Vee," I finally replied, "but imagine what would happen if I told Mama that I wanted to marry you. Although she likes you, she'd say that it's too soon. I'm just starting out with my career."

"You don't have to tell her anything. We'll just organise two friends as witnesses and sign the papers. Then, later, we can go and file for divorce."

"I understand, but you know that I'm not allowed to work in the legal profession if I've committed a crime. Suppose our secret blows up? I'll be in deep shit," I argued.

"But no one will find out."

"Well, you never know, Vee," I said, "but for a good friend like you I think I'm willing to take the risk."

"Did I hear you right? Did you say you'll do it?" she asked excitedly.

Vee squeezed me in a long, warm hug and kissed my forehead.

"But this marriage will just be a sham to get you citizenship, right?"

"Yes," she said, nodding.

"Well, then I'll be happy to be your husband in inverted commas."

"I'll count on you, Bafana," she said with a smile.

An hour after Vee had left, Sergeant Nkuna from the Protea Magistrate's Court called me to say that three guys who had been arrested for public drinking the night before wanted some legal representation. Since I had handled Zero's case we had come to a gentleman's agreement that for every client he gave me he would receive a commission of R100.

* * *

That night there was a power cut that affected most parts of Soweto, including Bara Hospital. The newspapers all reported the matter differently in the morning. Some said that there had been a cable theft, some said that the old substation in Orlando East had collapsed, but what they all agreed on was that at Bara Hospital the back-up generators had also failed. Most of the patients at Bara Hospital, including my uncle, were transferred to other hospitals, such as Helen Joseph and Coronation, west of Johannesburg, but my uncle wasn't lucky that night. He died in the ambulance on his way to one of the hospitals.

TWENTY-SIX
Sunday, February 20

It was a Sunday morning. The day of my uncle's funeral. It was a very hot day and Mama and her uncles, whom I had never seen before, had hired a big tent to accommodate all the mourners who had come to pay their last respects to Uncle Nyawana. The tent was spread right in the middle of our street in Chi, and both entrances to the street had been completely closed off.

Strangely, the coffin was inside the tent as the elders had finally agreed, after some discussion, that the corpse could not come inside the yard. That was because my uncle had not died of natural causes, and the elders believed that if the corpse entered the yard it would spell further misfortune for my family.

A sad hymn was sung in Sesotho to commence the proceedings. It was the first time in my life that a hymn had made me feel afraid. It was almost as if dead people were singing it.

Modimo ore file sebakanyana   (God has given us this little time,)
sena,
Le motsotsonyana.   (And this second.)

If it had not been for the coffin in the middle of the tent and the Avbob hearse, a passer-by would have easily mistaken the over-perfumed and overdressed mourners for a fashion parade.

Mama was sitting between sis Zinhle and Uncle Thulani. She was wearing a black maternity dress and a beret of the same colour. Uncle Thulani himself was in a black single-breasted jacket, a brushed checked shirt, striped trousers and Grasshopper casual lace-ups. Sis Zinhle looked immaculate in her black panel skirt, with leopard-print belt, and striped cowl neck. In the same row of hired, grey plastic chairs sat my sister Nina, sis Dudu and her daughter, Palesa, as well as other people that considered themselves family. Nina was wearing a long-sleeved black mesh top, beige leather jacket and black twill pants.

All the family members occupied about five rows in the tent. Uncle Guava's former girlfriends and their children were also there, but Uncle Guava was still in jail because the prison authorities had refused to grant him permission to come and bury his brother.

I was sitting in the fourth row with Vee, who was wearing a geometric V-neck tunic, wide denim jeans and camel casual shoes. The other people in our row were Zero, Dilika, Bunju, PP and some other people who, I decided, were only masquerading as concerned relatives to benefit from the after tears that would be held immediately after the funeral. Most of the people around us smelt of alcohol and it was obvious that Zero, PP and Dilika hadn't slept the previous night. They had probably been drinking under the tent during the night-time vigil.

As I was thinking this, another hymn was started in Zulu and Priest Mthembu stood up.

| Abanye bayangale, | (Others are going that side,) |
| Abanye bayawela. | (Others are crossing.) |

Priest Mthembu raised his right hand to stop the singing before he began to preach from his Bible. He was wearing a checked shirt and paisley tie, and two-pleat black formal trousers which had very sharp creases ironed into them. He asked us to close our eyes as he prayed for us, but I didn't.

"Father, You taught us that the dead are not absent. Father, know our difficulties and our needs. The loss of our beloved brother, Uncle and father, was tragic and unexpected. In Your love we are able to overcome all things. Lord, grant us the grace to meet our responsibilities with strength." He paused and wiped away the sweat that was streaming down his face, but his eyes were still closed. "All-powerful and merciful Father," he raised his voice and swung his right hand in the air, "in the death of Christ You have opened a gateway to eternal life. Look mercifully on our brother. He had suffered enough on this earth. Lord God, it is Your will that we imitate Your Son by loving those who speak or act against us. Help us to observe the commandments; returning good for evil and learning to forgive as Your Son forgave those who persecuted Him. Amen!"

As soon as Priest Mthembu sat down the mourners started to sing a popular Zulu hymn:

Amagugu alelizwe	(The heritage of this world)
Azophele'mathuneni.	(Will end at the grave.)
Seng'yahamba,	(Now I'm going,)
Ngiyolala.	(I'm going to rest.)

As if they shared one drunken brain, PP, Dilika and Zero were chanting their own demonic chorus to the rhythm of the hymn.

Amagwebu alebiya	(The foam of this beer)
Azophele'bodleleni.	(Will end in the bottle.)
Seng'yahamba,	(Now I'm going,)
Ngiyolala ngidakiwe.	(I'm going to rest, I'm drunk.)

For the next item on the programme, friends and relatives were asked to come and speak about the deceased.

My sister's boyfriend, Bheki, was the MC and he called PP to come and talk about my uncle. PP was wearing checked frontier trousers, a corduroy blazer, a peach poplin shirt and brown formal shoes. I watched him as he stood next to my uncle's coffin, balancing his drunken body by holding onto the side of it. In his right hand he was carrying the programme which contained my uncle's picture and his history.

"The death of my friend, bra Nyawana here, was a dream come true for him. I mean, he knew that one day he was going to die like most of us will of Aids or hunger here ekasi." He stopped, belched, and pointed randomly at the mourners. "I knew the deceased from toeka when we were still in primary sgele. We used to be bullies. We stole pencils and lunchboxes from other student moegoes. That was when he still had both legs. We once stole a nip of J&B whisky from our teacher Mrs Kubheka's handbag and drank it at the back of the class while she was teaching. That is why, even when he was hit by the faulty cricket on New Year's Day, J&B was still our favourite ugologo. All in all, bra Nyawana was the man. I remember him once keeping seven girlfriends at once . . ." He belched again and looked at the coffin. "Bra Nyawana, my bra, I say rest in *pieces* now. I'm hoping that God will stand your noise in heaven because you were very talkative here on earth, my bra. Good luck in heaven!"

There was laughter as PP staggered back towards his seat.

For the next item on the programme all the family members and friends were asked to come and look at the deceased in the coffin for one last time.

Surprisingly, Vee refused to come up, although Mama regarded her as part of the family, and I found that Bunju was behind me in the queue. She was wearing an exotic blue denim skirt and a sleeveless Calvin Klein T-shirt. Although her thighs were thick, she looked gorgeous.

Bunju took only one look at my deceased uncle's expressionless face and burst into tears. She cried so loudly that everybody in the tent looked at her.

"I warned you all that people with weak hearts must not come over here," said Priest Mthembu.

Still with tears on her face, Bunju lowered her head onto my chest, threw her arms round me and sobbed. Bunju hardly knew my uncle, but I guess she was shocked to see a dead body inside the coffin. I gave her a long hug, but my eyes were searching the crowd for Zero.

"This is a request to the driver of the red BMW with numberplate BMT 147 GP," announced Bheki, as I spotted Zero in the third row, and I tried to push Bunju away. "Please remove your car from the driveway where you have parked. The owner of the house wants to come out and he's late for work."

Out of the blue, most of the guys sitting in my row and the one behind jingled their keys in the air as if they were the owners of the red BMW. Even the heavily drunk man sitting next to Dilika, whose unhealthy aroma seemed to creep from under his orange overalls, jingled his Yale padlock keys in the air, to the amusement of the beautiful girls behind him.

But the owner of the car happened to be PP and he stood up and staggered out of the tent.

* * *

At midday, the cortege left for Avalon Cemetery, which was just across the railway line behind Chiawelo Station.

Leading the cortege was the hearse. It honked its horn all the way to the cemetery. A limousine that was supposed to be for the family members followed, but it was so full with my so-called relatives, who had scrambled to be in it, that there was no room for the rest of us. The rest of the mourners were either in their own cars or inside the five grey Putco buses that had been hired by the undertakers for Mama. All the buses were full and some people were even hanging precariously from the doors.

My sister, Nina, was sitting next to me in the back seat of PP's BMW so that we could catch up on a few things. Her boyfriend, Bheki, was in sis Zinhle's car. They were driving just behind the limo as he had to be at the cemetery in time to MC.

As the BMW slowly followed the procession, Dilika poured some J&B whisky out of a bottle into the cap and swallowed. He then refilled it and passed it on to PP who was driving.

"I think Rea is mad," said PP, swallowing the whisky and returning the cap to Dilika. "I mean, how could she choose Avbob out of all the services that are available here ekasi? I think that bra Dingaan's Rose Funerals could have handled this funeral better, but Rea chose the Afrikaners!"

"Don't be a racist, so far they've handled it perfectly well," interjected Nina.

"You're still young, Nina," said PP, with no emotion registering in his eyes. "This undertaker will only bring more death here ekasi because the owners are racist AWB Afrikaners."

"Read my lips! You're right, bra PP," said Dilika. "The business should be given to kasi people. How will small black businesses grow if we don't support them?" He rubbed his bloodshot eyes.

"How can you say that?" responded Nina in a storm of bad temper. "How can you see my uncle's death as a business opportunity, huh? I thought you were his friends!"

"I think you're misunderstanding bra Dilika," said PP protectively. "All that he's saying is that Avbob is owned by whites who don't understand our culture."

"I haven't seen anything wrong with the way they're handling it," I said.

"I thought you'd understand because you've been to university, Advo," said PP, looking at me in the rear-view mirror. "Look at the name Avbob itself. You know what it stands for? The name is an abbreviation for Almal Vrek Behalwe Ons Boere. These Afrikaners are here in the township to continue what they have been doing for centuries: killing abodarkie. The only difference is that these days they're making a huge profit out of it because they kill you today and bury you tomorrow."

We all burst out laughing as PP took the bottle of J&B from Dilika and drank generously from it.

* * *

Lihle izulu,	(Heaven is beautiful,)
Ikhaya labaNgcwele,	(The home of the holy people,)
Lapho abaNgcwele	(Where the holy people)
Baphumula khona.	(They rest there.)

The Zulu hymn was sung by close to three hundred mourners that had come to the cemetery. About twenty different funerals were being held at the same time in Avalon Cemetery and, because of the lack of space, people were sitting and standing on top of the tombstones. Both Nina and I were scanning the faces of the mourners as PP drove past the cemetery looking for somewhere to park. Many of their faces were stamped with smiles and as PP parked his BMW, we saw a young guy in an expensive striped suit who hadn't even bothered to go into the cemetery. He stood by the boot of his new BMW. His laptop was open and it seemed like he was watching a movie.

"President Mbeki should do something about the way we attend funerals here in Soweto," said Nina as soon as we stepped out of PP's BMW. "I think that only the immediate relatives of the deceased should be allowed into the cemetery." She pointed at a huge crowd of mourners and said, "Look at how full this place is! Somehow, I don't think they all came here to pay their last respects to the deceased." She shook her head. "These people are just here to eat because they live in poverty."

As we entered the cemetery we saw Zero. He was wearing beige two-pleat formal trousers, a long-sleeved blue shirt and a brown double-breasted jacket. His head shone because of his new S-curl hairstyle. As we watched him, Zero's cellphone rang and he answered it, bellowing in his deep voice at the person on the other end of the line.

"Yes, you must come, kawu. Walala wasala! You snooze, you lose!" He paused. "Yes, food and ladies galore, mthakathi!" He paused again. "Yes . . . I'm staring at the cheesiest thing I've ever seen." He paused yet again, his eyes scanning the faces of the girls as they stood around the graveside. "I've never seen thighs as beautiful as these, kawu. Wait, let me describe her for you." He balanced his cellphone between his right shoulder and his ear. "She's a complete system with surround sound and loudspeakers." He paused to demonstrate the lady's curves with both hands. "I'm not joking, mthakathi, I'm siriyasi." He moved his hands behind him, nearly touching his own buttocks. "She has *serious consequences* as well, kawu. You're losing out. By the end of the funeral I know she'll be mine, mthakathi. There'll be an after tears back at the tent and I'll invite her over." He paused. "Fine then, mthakathi, I'll see you in the queue for food. Moja!"

By the graveside I stood between Zero and Nina. Most people were standing in silence with their heads bowed, but Zero was using the opportunity to flirt with the lady behind us who was holding a black umbrella.

"Hi, beautiful lady," he began in a subdued voice. "That dress looks nice on you. I wouldn't mind if you wore it to my mother's funeral."

"Thanks," responded the lady, her eyes bright with excitement.

"Don't worry, I'll give you my contacts after the service," he continued as Priest Mthembu opened the service with a short Zulu prayer.

"Nkosi, Jesu Kristo, ngokulala kwakho izinsuku ezintathu ethuneni wacwebisa amathuna abo bonke abakholwa kuwe," started Priest Mthembu, the sweat breaking out on his face. "Nakuba imizimba yabo ilele emihlabathini sinethemba kodwa lokuthi bayovuka. Sengathi umzalwane wethu lona angalala aphumule ngoxolo kulelithuna kuze kufike lolosuku oyomvusa ngalo, umngenise ekukhanyeni kwasezulwini. Amen!"

I looked at Mama and the other members of my family who were sitting under the small green tent by the graveside. The tears that I could see in her eyes didn't fall and I thought that she probably didn't have any more tears to cry, as she had cried a lot.

Koloi ya Eliya!	(Prophet Elijah's wagon!)
Hae duma yatsamaya!	(When it roars, it's time to go!)
Lenna ke ya rata ho bona mangeloi,	(I also want to see the angels,)
Thabeng tsa Sione le bahalaledi.	(At the mountains of Zion with the holy people.)

The mourners sang the Sesotho hymn as the coffin was lowered into the grave. Priest Mthembu asked the family members to come forward and throw a little earth into the grave before all the mourners were given the opportunity to do the same.

"Oh! Hamba kahle, sihlobo sethu, usuphumile osizini lwalomhlaba; sowuye'khaya le ezulwini, kuBaba wethu okubizile," Priest Mthembu preached as I stepped forward. "Nakhu sikhala izinyembezi sesibuhlungu, ngoba sesikwamukiwe; kodwa intando kaBaba wethu mayidunyiswe ngezikhathi zonke. Usiphindele lapho wathatshathwa khona. Sal'usulala la elibeni, uze uvuke ngolokugcina. Sesicela kuNkulunkulu; akuhawukele akungenise ekukhanyeni kwasezulwini."

I was the first one to take some of the earth from the spade Zero was holding by the graveside. As I did so, I noticed that his eyes were angled towards a group of ladies as if he were selecting potential wives from amongst them. Mama, Nina and sis Dudu started to cry behind me as I threw the earth into the grave. As soon as they had done the same, Mama collapsed in the arms of a male elder with a double chin whom I didn't know while Nina fell into my arms.

Then it was the turn of all the township mourners. They took turns to put soil into the grave using shovels and spades. Among the mourners I saw the old man Sekoto, the neighbours whose house Uncle Guava had burnt down, and maTau, the woman who had come to make peace with my uncle around Christmas time. I knew in my heart that the only reason they'd come to the funeral was to make sure that my uncle was really dead.

Priest Mthembu introduced the old man with the double chin as the deceased's uncle and a representative of the Kuzwayo family. I had never met the man before, but I found out later that he was a brother of my grandfather from KwaZulu-Natal. The man stood up to give the final word.

"We, the Kuzwayos, want to thank all of you for accompanying my nephew to his last resting place. We thank you for showing us that death is not a private horror. Without you all, we could not have managed. Therefore we would like to ask you, all of you, to come and join us for something to eat. Thank you!"

* * *

Placed in the gateless driveway of our home were two big steel baths full of dirty water. Everyone who came from the cemetery was required to wash their hands and erase all thoughts of death and human decay as they did so. Perhaps a hundred mourners had arrived before us and washed their hands. Some of them were already eating, while others made up three long queues for the food.

Vee came to tell me that she couldn't stay any longer as she was on night shift at the hospital. She hadn't come to the cemetery as she had been busy helping with the preparation of food for the mourners. Uncle Thulani was also leaving to prepare for his night shift at Sun City and he agreed to take Vee to the taxis on the Old Potch Road in his yellow Beetle.

Behind me as I stood in the queue for food I could hear PP teasing someone. He sounded drunk.

"Ah, old man," said PP in a loud voice. "I think God has probably forgotten about you. He only punishes the young nowadays. I hope oorla bra Nyawana will remind God of your existence, madala, because you're the reason we don't have enough meat at this funeral."

Most people in the queue laughed. When I looked back I saw that the old man was Mr Sekoto.

"Hey, you women in the kitchen, listen up!" PP called out loudly. "Don't give old people like this one meat with bones! Give them the fat. They have been to enough funerals here in Soweto over the years and now they must give young people a chance to eat."

Most people laughed at PP's joke, including Zero, who was immediately behind him in the queue, an empty plastic plate in his hand.

"You know, bra PP," said Zero, "I think God has a very strange sense of humour. How can He kill good people like bra Nyawana and spare all the useless people here in Chi?"

Dilika appeared a moment later carrying a brown plastic plate heaped with rice, pap, mashed potato, pumpkin, beetroot, cabbage, salad and meat. His mouth was already filled to capacity and, as he spoke, pieces of food sprang out of it and landed on PP's nose.

"Hey, bra PP and Zero, are you still here?" he asked in a surprised tone of voice. "Read my lips! This is my third plate and if you're not careful, the pots are going to be empty by the time you get there. Bra Nyawana was our best buddy and we deserve the best treatment from those women in the kitchen. Stop standing here in the queue and go in there and get the special food. Go!" he commanded loudly as he chased away a big green fly that had just settled on his plate.

Hurriedly, PP and Zero left the queue.

"And don't forget to ask for lots of meat," added Dilika.

After a little while PP came back holding a plate of rice, pap, red meat, chicken, salad and beetroot. As he passed close to me he stopped and looked at Verwoerd who was sitting and panting on the floor next to the tent, watching the mourners eat. As he stood there, Bunju threw a bone and Verwoerd immediately jumped up and caught it.

"Hey, Bunju," PP called out loudly. "Do you know why the dog chose to sit next to you?"

"I don't know, but I guess it's because I'm the only one giving him food," she responded innocently.

PP smiled kindly as if he were softening the words that he was about to say.

"No, dear, don't compliment yourself on your kind heart. Verwoerd chose you because you're eating off *his* plate. His owner, oorla bra Nyawana, used to feed him from that plate every day. That I know for sure."

Bunju glanced at her plate as the people around her stared at her with amusement written on their faces.

202

PP continued walking towards the tent where Dilika and the others were drinking and eating. Bunju stared after him, looking as if she could happily plunge her long red fingernails into his back.

"I tell you, bra Dilika," PP said, gazing at the mourners that were eating hungrily under the tent, "most of the stomachs here today aren't used to meals like this. They're used to snoek, amagwinya, iskhambane and nzo. Yeah, that's their kasi diet."

PP was loud and unpleasant, but most of the people in the tent still laughed at whatever he said.

In the tent our big black rubbish bin had been turned into a refrigerator; it was full of beers and ciders that had been buried under an avalanche of ice. I sat down and listened to the kasi gossip: the latest victim of Aids, who was sleeping with whose wife, who recently got employed or married, who recently won the fah-fee. As always, PP was the one doing most of the talking.

"You can tell me fokkol about DK Extension," he said, leaping up from his chair. "Diepkloof Extension is the kasi for chizboys, bhujwas and amakoporosh who speak English through their noses to sound like abongamla. Yeah, they're all fakes there! Tell me about a rough kasi like Gomorrah and I'll verstaan." He paused to collect his thoughts. "Anyway, Alexandra is the real kasi, Baba. I used to blom there at the corner of Ten and Hofmeyr Streets, opposite the church. I was the leader of a gang and people used to call me Havoc. We did everything from hijacking to robbing banks," he said. "We also used to break into rich white people's houses in suburbs like Sandton and Morningside, Baba. Where do you think I got these tattoos from, huh? I got them edanyani, Baba! Seven years!" PP lifted the five fingers on his one hand to indicate seven.

As he was speaking, I looked hard at his scarred face. The new rumour circulating ekasi was that he had survived torture by some heartless white policemen who had been trying to get him to tell them the names of his collaborators in a bank robbery. It was said that PP had been tied inside a sack with a live cat and, together, he and the cat were thrown into Hartebeespoort Dam near Magaliesburg. The poor cat was so afraid that it started to scratch PP's face. PP's hands were tied behind his back, but after a fight that lasted for about ten minutes, he managed to kill the animal with his teeth. It was also rumoured that he had used the money he had stolen from the bank to build his business empire.

"Do you guys know why I left Gomorrah?" asked PP, holding his glass of whisky in one hand and a piece of meat in the other. "I left twelve years ago because I killed Gintsa, the leader of a gang called Triple O. Out Of Order. His buddies were after me and I had to run to my aunt in Mambisa. That was before I came to live in Chi."

We were still swallowing PP's lies when Priest Mthembu came out of the house. He had taken off his jacket, but he was still in his shirt and waistcoat. As he reached the tent, he ran his forefinger around the inside of his mouth to remove a piece of meat that seemed to be stuck somewhere between his teeth.

While he did this Zero opened his Hansa beer with his teeth and threw the bottle top on the floor, which was already littered with bottle tops, bones, cigarette butts and greasy plastic plates and spoons. Priest Mthembu looked at all the drunkards and shook his grey head.

"If we could commit ourselves to sport like we've committed ourselves to drinking alcohol and smoking cigarettes, then I tell you,

204

my children, Bafana Bafana would win the next World Cup in South Korea," he said.

"Don't worry, Baba Mfundisi! Read my lips, drunkenness is necessary for us while we mourn our beloved friend," said Dilika, his forefinger fishing around in his nostril.

Priest Mthembu left the tent slowly, his eyes still on us as if he were witnessing the beginning of an imminent township tragedy.

"I miss my bra Nyawana, he was a taaikop that one," said PP, holding his glass of J&B. "I remember we argued a lot about dying in December last year. I told him that he would die first and he didn't believe me, but look what happened. He died and he still owes me the R1 000 that he borrowed from me to bet on fah-fee."

"Don't worry about that, bra PP," said Dilika, pointing at me. "Read my lips! His laaitie, Advo, will repay you with interest because he's a big advocate."

"What I'm concerned about is that we didn't bury our bra according to his wishes," said Zero. "Remember that bra Nyawana once said that he would like to be buried face down and naked so that the whole kasi would be able to kiss his arse on Judgement Day? I'm afraid he'll come back as a ghost to haunt us."

"I can't believe I won't see bra Nyawana again. Read my lips! That man cheated death several times. He always survived because he was so stubborn. That was until that faulty cricket prepared the way for him on New Year's Day," said Dilika.

"That man was first class at rolling a zol," said PP. "That's what I'm going to miss the most about him. To oorla bra Nyawana Jabulani Kuzwayo!"

Everyone in the tent watched as PP poured a little bit of his J&B

on the ground and went down on all fours. It was a demonstration of brotherhood that I had never seen at any after tears before.

"Wherever you are, drink a bit of this to give you courage, nkalakatha. I'm not being stingy, but I won't give you much because we're running low on supplies, my bra," he said, as if talking to my uncle face to face. "I also don't want you to arrive in heaven drunk, you know how bra Jesu and God are, They'll kick you back to hell here in the kasi if you turn up smelling of whisky."

"Sure, Nyawana, nkalakatha, we'll miss you," said Zero, pouring a bit of his Hansa beer on the ground.

"Bra Nyawana, mfethu," said Dilika, also pouring a little bit of his J&B on the ground. "Read my lips! I'll miss you! I say to you now, RIP. Return If Possible."

TWENTY-SEVEN
Tuesday, February 29

About a week after my uncle's funeral I was at our Chi home when Mama and sis Zinhle arrived. Mama wanted to introduce me to the people who had bought the house before I left for my office, as well as begin the process of moving some of our things to Naturena. My uncle didn't own much and if it hadn't been for his old bed, I'm sure everything he owned would have fitted in the boot of sis Zinhle's car, but Mama had decided that everything was to be stored in the garage until she finally decided what to do with it. I was sure that she would either give his things away to Aunty Manto, or to the people that knocked at the door for old clothes every week.

"As I was telling you, chomza," sis Zinhle said to Mama as we packed my late uncle's dirty clothes into the two sports bags that Mama had brought with her, "I think I know why your brother didn't recover after the accident."

"Oh, yes?" said Mama, folding a T-shirt and putting it inside one of the sports bags.

"A nurse confided in me that it was because the hospital prescribed the wrong medication for him. I think that since Bafana is now a lawyer, he must sue them. You must take this matter forward, chomza, because if it wasn't for their negligence, your brother would not even have been on life-support in the first place," she observed.

"But, chomza, how could something like that happen?" Mama asked with a puzzled face. "Those nurses told me that his wounds were so severe that there was no way he could have survived, especially given the fact that he was asthmatic."

"Believe me, chomza, those are all lies. I heard that the hospital didn't even know that he was asthmatic."

"Seriously, chomza?" asked Mama.

"Vele!"

"That bloody hospital!" Mama cursed. "When did you hear this?"

"Yesterday, when I was on duty at Harriet Shezi."

"You're right, we'll have to sue them." She turned to me for affirmation. "You see, Bafana! We must do it soon, while the matter is still fresh."

By now the room smelt very bad and Mama went to the window to open it. She put her face outside as if she were sucking a lungful of air.

"Yes, I think you must," continued sis Zinhle. "You must sue the Gauteng MEC for Health. I'm sure Bafana knows about these things. The hospital is sued almost every day for taking people's lives unnecessarily."

"Those bloody people will know me! We must prepare the papers."

"Yes, chomza!"

About thirty minutes later the new owners of our house knocked at the door. They were a middle-aged man and his overweight wife. Mama introduced the new owners of our house as Mr and Mrs Zwane. The woman's round face was glowing with a smile, but she was breathing heavily. As she sat on our old sofa it sunk down because of her weight. Mama, sis Zinhle and I looked at each other without a word as the springs of the old sofa creaked. We all expected it to break at any moment. Luckily, her husband started to talk and distracted us.

"Me and my wife here have decided that we should come and occupy the house soon, as the papers have already gone through," said Mr Zwane.

"When were you thinking of moving in?" Mama asked.

"Well, as soon as you have finished removing all your belongings," said Mr Zwane, looking at his wife. "How long do you think it will take you to do that?"

"Give us two more days."

"Two days is fine. We'll come on Friday to get the keys from you."

"Not a problem. I'll leave another set at my son's office by the BP Garage at Mangalani, just in case you come early."

Mr Zwane and his wife left after I had given them my cellphone number and directions to my office, but the sofa remained pressed down from where Mrs Zwane had been sitting on it long after she had gone.

Mama, sis Zinhle and I went back to my uncle's room and continued packing his stuff. As Mama and sis Zinhle were talking about Mrs Zwane's weight, Verwoerd slunk into my uncle's room and looked at us. He had lost so much weight that his bones had crept to the surface. Mama took one look at him and decided that he too should come and live with us in Naturena.

Later, as she was taking the last of the things she wanted from the house to sis Zinhle's car, Mama opened the door to the room that used to be mine.

"You also don't have many things in here, Bafana," said Mama, standing at the door. "I've organised a van for the beds and wardrobes. They'll be here tomorrow morning, but today I want to do all the washing. You must put all your dirty clothes in that bag. I want to test my new washing machine," she announced proudly.

"So, you bought a new washing machine at last?" I asked.

"It's a beautiful one," she answered excitedly. "You'll see, it's automatic, all you do is press a button and it does the job for you."

After locking the doors to the house we all got into sis Zinhle's car. I sat in the back seat with the clothing and bags. Sis Zinhle had offered to drop me at Protea Magistrate's Court, as I had an assault case that was due to start at ten o'clock that morning.

As I climbed out of the car sis Zinhle offered to come pick me up after my case had finished at about twelve, but I declined.

"Don't forget to load Verwoerd in the van when you come to Naturena tomorrow," Mama reminded me.

As soon as Mama and sis Zinhle had left, I walked towards the holding cells where I was to meet Sergeant Nkuna, but on my way there my cellphone rang. It was Vee.

"Bee, I just wanted to remind you that we are meeting at ten this Friday at the registry office on the corner of Harrison and Plein."

"Okay, I'll be there."

"Don't forget to bring your ID and birth certificate with you."

"Fine."

"Our marriage ceremony is at half past ten."

"Okay, Vee. Listen, I'll speak to you later. My case is starting soon."

Immediately after the call I felt scared at the thought of our marriage, but at the same time I knew I needed the money to sustain my business.

I spotted Sergeant Nkuna. He was smiling and waving at me as I approached. Everything at the Protea Magistrate's Court had become routine. I always started by giving Sergeant Nkuna his R100 commission for getting me a client, then I went and talked to the magistrate that was handling the case in his office, then I went to the prosecutor and the arresting officer before appearing in the court to plead guilty or not guilty on behalf of my client. Thereafter my clients would be let out, either on bail or after paying a fine.

At about quarter to twelve I left the Magistrate's Court after securing the release of my client with a fine of R1 000. I stopped a taxi at the gate, but got off ten minutes later at my office by the BP Garage. I bought some lunch and went to my office. Yomi was there with a bunch of customers that had come to use the public phones and the internet, but he didn't see me enter as I used the other door.

That afternoon as I was busy reading my e-mails, sis Zinhle arrived with two bottles of champagne. I looked at sis Zinhle. She was dressed formally in her black pants, black jacket and white shirt, as if she was trying to impress her wealthy boyfriend.

"I have come to personally congratulate you as I heard that you won your case this morning," she said in her angelic voice. "Today we must celebrate in style."

She went to the door and locked it. When she returned she put her hand on my shaven head and gently kissed me on my neck. I felt a shudder run through me. A moment later my mouth was shaping hers in a kiss as my left hand covered her breast.

TWENTY-EIGHT
Friday, March 3

The taxi dropped me at the corner of Bree and Harrison Streets at about ten in the morning. The hawkers along Harrison Street's congested pavement looked at me with envy as I was wearing my formal black suit, a black tie and a white shirt. Before I could even enter the Home Affairs building, at the corner of Plein Street, a couple of hawkers flashed their cameras in my face in an attempt to strike a photo deal with me. I ignored them and entered the building, groping inside my jacket pocket to make sure that my identity document and birth certificate were still there.

My marriage ceremony with Vee was only due to begin at half past ten, but I knew she had been waiting for me since quarter to. I passed the security staff at the entrance and stopped at the steps for a while to take a breath. My mind was still split over whether I should go through with the marriage. As I weighed my options my cellphone rang. It was Mama.

"Where are you, Bafana?" she asked, sounding angry.

"Ehh . . . I'm in the city."

"I know you're in the city, Yomi told me. Where in the city?"

"Ehhh . . . I'm here on Plein Street."

"Why are you hesitant? Don't you even know where you are?"

"I'm at Home Affairs and I'll be back in about an hour, Mama."

For the first time in my life Mama clicked her tongue and dropped the phone on me. I looked at the time as I put my phone on vibrate. It was already twenty minutes past ten. Vee must be panicking up there, I thought, as I walked towards the lift on the ground floor. I pressed the button to call the lift, waited for half a second, then quickly used the stairs to the first floor.

Vee was waiting for me on one of the benches outside a large room and, as I came up the stairs, she smiled joyfully at me. I couldn't resist the pleasure of eyeing my bride. She looked gorgeous in her striped black pants, yellow shirt and puffy black jacket. We hugged each other before we walked into the large room where our marriage would take place.

Mr Khumalo, our marriage officer, had just come in, having just finished officiating at another couple's marriage. It was twenty-five minutes past ten and our marriage ceremony was due to start in five minutes.

"Do you have a ring on you?" he asked after Vee had introduced us.

Vee looked at me as I pretended to be searching my pockets even though I knew that I didn't have a ring on me.

"No problem," said Mr Khumalo in a sympathetic voice. "It's not compulsory to have one, but I recommend it. I can give you five minutes to get one. If you go down the hall to Room 107 you'll see a lady selling rings there."

As I paid for the ring, which cost me R250, I was thinking about the R15 000 Vee had promised me. I needed it to add to the R7 000 that was all that was left between me and poverty.

When I came back to the large room where the marriage ceremony was to take place, Vee had already organised two witnesses. They were the couple that was to be married immediately after us.

At exactly twenty-four minutes to eleven, Mr Khumalo began the ceremony. As he did so, my phone began to vibrate inside my pocket and my guilt at what I was about to do began to grow to an alarming size in my mind.

A second later I heard a familiar voice shouting at the door. It echoed throughout the hall and disturbed the proceedings.

"What do you think you're doing, Bafana?" Mama shouted as she burst into the room, a fiery rage in her eyes. "I've been looking for you all over the place and then they tell me that you're in here! Marrying someone without my knowledge? You're evil, Bafana! A demon!"

The marriage office suddenly became very hot as I saw Mama waddle through the door in the company of Yuri and sis Zinhle. By now she was seven months pregnant, but at that moment she looked old and ugly.

"Sies! You're a disgrace, Bafana," chorused sis Zinhle in an even sharper tone of voice, squinting maliciously at Vee.

A shock wave passed visibly through Mr Khumalo as he took in the situation.

"You'll be the death of me, Bafana," Mama finally said. "What's this?" She waved a piece of paper in my face.

It was my real statement of results from UCT. I had been looking for it since it had gone missing before Christmas. Mama must have found it in the pocket of one of my pairs of trousers she was washing in her new washing machine.

"There must be some mistake, I can –"

But Mama's composure had completely disintegrated and, before I could say anything else, she fired a warm klap on my left cheek. The two witnesses burst into wild laughter and the marriage officer shook his head in sympathy, but Mama continued to shout at me.

"I'm not a fool, Bafana!" she said, twitching her nostrils in rage. "I called UCT this morning and they confirmed that you had failed. Why did you lie to me, Bafana, huh?" she asked, and started to weep.

"I'm sorry, Mama, I . . ."

But there was no way I could defend my lies.

"Is it true, Bee?" Vee sniffled.

"Yes, he was a very nice boy until he began associating with you foreigners," said sis Zinhle, looking at Vee with hatred.

"I don't know you any more and I don't trust you either!" Mama said, sobbing up great lumps of pain. "You're a bad boy and I don't want anything to do with you. You hear me, Bafana, huh?"

This time I kept quiet. Feelings of failure, guilt and exposure battled furiously in my head. I needed to escape it all as quickly as possible. I needed to escape Mama and sis Zinhle and Vee.

Making up my mind, I ran past Mama, sis Zinhle and Yuri towards the stairs. Mama clapped her hands in horror.

"You're not my son any more, you hear me?" she shouted as I ran past her. "You are not my son any more!"

TWENTY-NINE
Tuesday, May 9

Two months after I had started my self-imposed exile in Diepsloot squatter camp, north of Johannesburg, I found myself at Germiston Station waiting for the Shosholoza Meyl to whisk me away from the blinding Jo'burg lights. As I waited for the train, my mind wandered over everything that had happened to me.

The evening after Mama had confronted me at Home Affairs, I had called Yomi to tell him what had happened. He had told me that Mama had also caused a scene in front of everyone at the office. Yomi had agreed to remove all my certificates from the walls of my office and bring them to his flat in Yeoville. The first night I had crashed at Yomi's place, but in the morning Yomi had suggested that I move in with his friend Tolu in Diepsloot, as no one would know me there.

The two months that I spent hiding at Tolu's place in Diepsloot squatter camp, operating the public telephones and working in the spaza shop, had quickly taught me that this was not what I wanted to end up doing with my life. Eventually, after I had agreed to pay him half the remaining money in my bank account, Yomi had given me the name and address of a friend of his who stayed in Point Road in Durban. That's where I was going. I was hoping that Durban was going to offer me a new lease of life. I had convinced myself that I didn't deserve to suffer any more and, with my degree certificate and statement of results on me, I thought I was ready to move on.

As the train left Germiston Station, at about half past seven in the evening, I opened my bottle of J&B whisky. Through the window, I stared out into the fading evening light, thinking of my bad fortune, which was unquestionably well deserved. No one had been able to track me down in Diepsloot as I had changed my cellphone number, but I could still read my e-mails from the internet café at Diepsloot Library. As I swallowed my second tot from the cap, I thought of the long e-mails that I had received from Vee and Nina over the last two months.

Vee had been deported back to Zimbabwe after failing to secure her work permit, and she was now working on the idea of going to London. She wasn't angry with me, so she said, but she wanted to know how I'd been able to hoodwink everyone about my results.

Nina's recent e-mails had begged me to come back home immediately. According to Nina, Mama never told anyone what had happened between us and now that we had a baby brother, Mama had cooled off slightly. He had been born a week earlier and he still had no name. She wondered if I had a beautiful name that I could give him.

Nina also briefed me about what had happened in the township during my absence. She told me that Dilika was still a drunkard, but PP had suddenly become very ill and bedridden. The rumour circulating in the township was that he had Aids. Meanwhile, sis Zinhle had reconciled with her husband.

By the time the train left Newcastle Station, at about twenty minutes to midnight, my whisky bottle was half empty. The whisky had freed me from the tension in my mind and, before the train reached Ladysmith, I fell asleep and dreamt of my uncle and his dog, Verwoerd. Verwoerd was trying to maul me, just as he had the first day I had come back to Chi from UCT, while my uncle, Mama, sis Zinhle, PP, Zero, Dilika, Vee, Bunju, Nina and uBaba Mfundisi stood around laughing.

Glossary

abodarkie – plural of "darkie"

abomabhebeza – plural of "mabhebeza"

abomahlalela – plural of "mahlalela"

abomashonisa – plural of "mashonisa"

abongamla – plural of "ngamla"

Almal Vrek Behalwe Ons Boere – everyone dies except us boers

amagwinya – bread dough fried in cooking oil (vetkoek)

amakoporosh – plural of "koporosh"

amakwere-kwere – plural of "kwere-kwere"

amanqina – cooked sheep's or cow's feet

amasethole – traditional Zulu medicine

amasimba! – shit!

a-ye-ye – warning call, alerting somebody of looming danger

baba/ubaba – originally "father", but used as an endearment for a friend

babuelli basechaba – people's representatives, normally referring to lawyers that offer people free legal aid

belofte – promise

bhujwa – derived from "bourgeoise", refers to a person from a middle-class / upper-class family

bleksem - bliksem

blom – stay/live

bra – buddy/mate

Chi – Chiawelo, also known as Tshiawelo

chizboy – a person from a sound financial background, used interchangeably with "bhujwa"

clipa – R100

cricket – firecracker

darkie – African person

diketo – a game using pebbles, played by kids in the street

Dudlu! Khula sihlahla sizodla'mapentshisi! – Grow up, peach tree, so that we can eat the peaches!

dumpy – 340 ml beer bottle

dushis – coloured people

edanyani – in jail
ekasi – in the township
esgele/isgele/sgele – (at) school
ex-thiza – ex-teacher

Fong Kong – fake / pirated merchandise
four five – penis

garo – train
G-string BMW – BMW 3 series

idanyani – jail
ihlungunhlungu – traditional Zulu medicine
isgele – see "esgele"
isibotho – someone who drinks heavily and whose body / face has been affected by
    the alcohol
iskhambane – township word for "bunny chow"
izimbatata – type of traditional sandals made out of cut car tyres

kasi – township
kawu – friend
ke ije – "howzit going" in Igbo
koloi ya Eliya – translates directly as "Prophet Elijah's wagon"; in township slang it
    means that the person is about to die of Aids
koporosh – fake
kota – "bunny chow" in township slang; used interchangeably with "iskhambane"
Kuveve brandy – KWV brandy
kwere-kwere – derogatory term for an immigrant from elsewhere in Africa

mabhebeza – baby, term of endearment for a lady
(Jozi) maboneng – (Johannesburg) place of lights
madala – old man
Madlokovu – clan name for the Ngema family
magez'epompini – he who washes himself from the tap
mahlalela – unemployed person
majiyane – he who lies . . . or a lawyer
makoti – daughter-in-law / bride
makoya – real, genuine, from "real McCoy"
Mambisa – Thembisa
maMfundisi – wife of a preacher
mashonisa – loan shark
mbamba – an illegally brewed, raw liquor
mfanawam – my son, my boy

220

Mfundisi – preacher

mkhulu – old man / grandfather

mntwana – endearment for a beautiful girl, used interchangeably with "mabhebeza"

moegoes – fools

moja – all right

Msawawa – Soweto

mshana – nephew / my friend

msunukanyoko – swearword, equivalent to "motherfucker"

mthakathi – originally means witch, but is now used to refer to a friend, and can be used interchangeably with the word "kawu"

ngamla – white person

ngishisa bhe – I'm very hot

ngiyak'ncanywa, ntwana – I love you, my boy

ngiyinsimbi ayigobeki – I'm the steel rod that doesn't bend

ngudus – quarts of beer

nkalakatha – used to refer to a friend; similar to "kawu" and "mthakathi"

Nkosi yam! – My Lord!

ntwana – young boy

nwanne – "child of my mother" in Igbo

nzo – bread

oorla – derived from the Afrikaans "oorle" (oorlede), meaning late (already passed away)

ouledi – mother (from "old lady")

pozi – place

sek'shubile – warning of danger coming, like "a-ye-ye"

self-cater – masturbate

sester – sister

sgele – see "esgele"

shaya – hit

sheshisa – hurry up

siriyasi – serious

six nine – toilet (can also mean going to the toilet to urinate)

slim – clever

smiley – sheep's head

smokser – train hawker

snyman – person that sells dagga / a drug dealer

sparapara – staff riding

straight – 750 ml bottle of alcohol

Sun City – Johannesburg Prison, known in Jo'burg as Sun City, because of its modern facilities

taaikop – stubborn
taima – father (derived from old-timer)
toeka – a long time ago
traditional bio slim – marijuana
traditional Rolex – derogatory term for a goathide bracelet called "isiphandla" in Zulu,
    which, after a traditional Zulu ritual, is worn on the wrist like a watch
TY – Teyateyaneng

ubaba – see "baba"
ugelezile – you went to school
ugologo – whisky or brandy
ukumokola – bribing the people of the law
ukupeyta – enema
ukuphalaza – induces vomiting
umbimbi – traditional Zulu medicine
umdubu – traditional Zulu medicine
umkhayawam wase Thekwini – my homeboy from Durban
umkhele – traditional Zulu medicine
umunne – "child of my mother" in Igbo
umusuzwane – traditional Zulu medicine
uNyawana – derogatory name referring to a person with one leg
uswazi – traditional Zulu medicine
uyabandlulula – you discriminate
Uyabhema yini, mkhulu? – Do you smoke, old man?
uyagayana – s/he is generous

vader – prison warder (also "father" in Afrikaans)
vele – affirmation / of course
verstaan – understand
Vietnam – Naledi Extension in Soweto
voetsek, wena! – fuck off, you!
Vreega – Vereeniging

walala wasala – if you sleep you'll be left behind

zak – money
zozo – shack
zwakala hier – come here

Acknowledgements

I would like to thank Sylt Quelle in Rantum, Wester-land, Germany, for the Writers' Fellowship on the Isle of Sylt. Special thanks also go to: Sibongile Tito, for the law lessons; Achal Prabhala in Bangalore, India, for the use of the Newtown office and the PC; my brothers Dennis and Elvis Mhlongo, for the laptops; and Gugu Masango and Wonderboy Peters, for their great friendship.

NIQ MHLONGO was born in Soweto in 1973. His first novel, *Dog Eat Dog*, was published by Kwela Books in 2004 and awarded the Mar de Letras Prize in 2006. He has also published short stories in South Africa and abroad. *After Tears* is his second novel.